lifeforce

lifeforce

A NOVEL

Annie Rodriguez

GREEN PLACE BOOKS *Brattleboro, Vermont*

Printed in the United States

10 9 8 7 6 5 4 3 2 1

Green Writers Press is a Vermont-based publisher whose mission is to
spread a message of hope and renewal through the words and images we
publish. Throughout we will adhere to our commitment to preserving
and protecting the natural resources of the earth. To that end, a
percentage of our proceeds will be donated to environmental activist
groups and The Southern Poverty Law Foundation. Green Writers Press
gratefully acknowledges support from individual donors, friends, and
readers to help support the environment and our publishing initiative.
Green Place Books curates books that tell literary and compelling
stories with a focus on writing about place—these books are more
personal stories/memoir and biographies.

GREEN PLACE BOOKS   GREEN WRITERS press

Giving Voice to Writers & Artists Who Will Make the World a Better Place
Green Writers Press | Brattleboro, Vermont
www.greenwriterspress.com

ISBN: 978-0-9994995-3-5

COVER DESIGN BY ASHA HOSSAIN DESIGN, LLC

PRINTED ON PAPER WITH PULP THAT COMES FROM FSC (FOREST STEWARDSHIP COUNCIL)-CERTIFIED, MANAGED
FORESTS THAT GUARANTEE RESPONSIBLE ENVIRONMENTAL, SOCIAL, AND ECONOMIC PRACTICES BY LIGHTNING
SOURCE. ALL WOOD-PRODUCT COMPONENTS USED IN BLACK & WHITE OR STANDARD COLOR PAPERBACK BOOKS,
UTILIZING EITHER CREAM OR WHITE BOOKBLOCK PAPER, THAT ARE MANUFACTURED IN THE LAVERGNE,
TENNESSEE, PRODUCTION CENTER ARE SUSTAINABLE FORESTRY INITIATIVE® (SFI®) CERTIFIED SOURCING.

To Joseph Simmons Ohr, Jr., MD., RPh. (1964–2017)
and
Cynthia L. Sutton, PhD.

For my two angels, one in heaven and one on earth.
My incredible mentors and encouragers, I love you and
appreciate you more than you will ever know.

Acknowledgments

My sincere gratitude to:
Dr. Ohr, I will always be grateful for the life events that allowed us to cross paths. You restored my confidence and curiosity as a student, and my study of anatomy under you in three months will always be unparalleled even by the most gifted of professors. My teacher, mentor, and friend, I will always carry you in my heart.

Dr. Sutton, there are simply no words. Your advice, encouragement, and mentorship have carried me in moments where I thought all was lost as I saw my hard work go up in flames. Little did I know you were helping to guide me to even greater opportunities that I would have failed to see had I not been pushed into a corner. I will always be thankful that I have a shoulder to lean on when my load gets too heavy, and hope I get to appreciate our growing friendship for years to come.

Professor John Sarkissian and his wife, Janice Vitullo, for their help with the Latin translations and their ability to keep teaching me long after I graduated, I love you both!

Dr. Robert H. Baker (1923–2018) and his incredible family, for their encouragement, support, and their willingness to always engage in interesting and stimulating conversations.

Steve Eisner and Dede Cummings, for believing in this novel even in its infant stages, and pushing me to make it the novel I envisioned it could be.

Gregory Norris-Master, writer extraordinaire, for making me feel welcomed as a newbie, and for your unconditional help as a writer and encouragement as a friend! I adore you!

Peggy Moran, for being the first editor for *Lifeforce* and encouraging me to keep going.

Asha Hossain, for turning my ideas into a stunner cover—beautiful work!

The staff at Green Writers Press, especially Rose Alexandre-Leach, Sarah Ellis, and Hillary Brown, for pushing this book's boundaries to force me to grow it into the novel it became.

My friends at When Words Count: James, Robyn and Chris, Christine and Jack, Shabnam and Abhijat, Mike and Tom—thank you for your encouragement and words of wisdom! You guys are talented writers, supportive spouses, and amazing friends!

Charita Cole Brown, for being a master hugger and a great writing coach!

Rachel (McKay) Deligiorgakis, Vilma (Marku) Zinsteyn, and Erin (Gooch) Winters, for being some of my first writer friends and encouragers!

To my amazing family and friends for putting up with me through this process and pushing me forward, thank you!

To all of you and those who I failed to mention, my thanks.

lifeforce

Chapter 1

2009

"This is it. Come on, Gillian, you can do this," Gillian sighed, trying to calm herself as she sat down on the floor of the attic in her mother's house, soon to be her own. One year to go until she was eighteen. But she still didn't want it. It was her mother's house, according to her father's will. And her mother should be there, taking care of her.

"I'm seventeen, damn it! I deserve my mother, not some cranky vampire with temper tantrum problems," Gillian huffed.

She sat within a candle circle for the fifth time in two weeks. Hopefully, this time her mother would show up and hear her out. But even as she desperately tried to assure herself that this time would be different, she couldn't get rid of the feeling that prickled at the back of her mind:

She won't show.

Gillian cleared her throat, moving her head side to side in an attempt to relax her fast beating heart, and took a deep breath, concentrating on the cinnamon smell coming from the teddy bear sitting beside her and the refreshing breeze coming from the open window on her right. Anything that could help her disentangle herself from her own head and focus on her magic. The success of the spell and her subsequent strength depended on it, and this time, her sanity did as well.

"This has to work. I need you." Hopefully, her mother could hear her. She had to. She had no idea how much she was missed, how much her daughter needed her.

And how much of her lifeforce her daughter had spent already in all her failed attempts to summon her.

Her mother had no idea how much Gillian resented her for opting to die instead of accepting immortality; if she had, she could finish raising Gillian and share her magic and motherly wisdom forever. Now, Gillian's powers still not fully developed, she had to train from her mother's grimoire instead of her incredible magic mastery if her mother were still alive. This would only slow down Gillian's learning, and the full control of her powers.

Yeah, they would get to that . . . eventually. Of course, Addie would say don't do it, that her mother had a reason for not choosing immortality and instead choosing to die. Who did that? Who would? Choose pain over life, over her daughter? Well, she would find out soon enough . . . hopefully.

Gillian sighed, her head moving from side to side again as she tried to get her body to relax once more, her lips beginning the incantation from the grimoire of Bridget Cassidy, her mother, now right in front of her, its pages soft and worn from hours spent running her fingers along her mother's words.

Ex mundo voco te
Ego te mea vita mutuo dono
Ex barathro
Revertere ad me

From my world I call to you
My life I loan you
From the netherworld
return to me

Gillian took a deep breath as she took the teddy bear into her hands. She coughed as the strong smell of cinnamon caught her right under her nostrils. But she wouldn't let that deter her. She pressed the fuzzy creature against her chest and closed her eyes.

Come on, Mom!

Gillian felt her heart rate speed up as she felt her hands tremble. Magic came at a cost. Her energy, her lifeforce, always got depleted as a result of magical utilization. Only practice could make her lifeforce more resistant to energy depletion; only rest could restore it. But despite the consequences, a weakening of her body for a time, she could not deny the thrill that came from using magic. The feeling of knowing that even though she possessed mortality, a time clock if you will, she held the upper hand when she used magic, a knowledge that no immortal, to her knowledge, possessed. Because even though she had heard of other witches as far back as ancient times, thanks to her mother's book of sorcery, she had never heard of a witch who possessed immortality. That would be against magic's rules, according to the grimoire. Therefore, magic was a gift only mortals could possess. And for someone being raised by a temperamental, immortal creature, one who was only too happy to remind her, and often, that she didn't have immortality's "protection," she would take anything she could get. And magic, when used properly, presented her with no simple—no ordinary—upper hand.

Her light strawberry blond hair whooshed as it moved with the force that her magic garnered, the color tossing between darker strawberry blond and honeyed tones, a sign that her magic was testing how far it could go.

Her mother had told her at the beginning of her magic journey that her sun-kissed blond hair would get darker the more powers she mastered, and in doing so, gave a teenager one more excuse to look in the mirror. It had been fun for a while, as her light blond became dirtied, honeyed, and light strawberry blond. But the more powers she thought she mastered, the more the hair-color changing stalled. And, well, so did her mirror time. She didn't need a reminder that her magic was going nowhere.

Just like the present attempt.

She was giving it all she had. And she could feel it taking a toll on her. After all, witchcraft was now, and had been since her birth, tied to her life, to her soul. The spells took a toll on her strength, on her lifeforce. And this time was no exception. She could only hope her strength would improve as she became more efficient and better at mastering her powers. That was her hope, her goal.

But today, she could feel her weakness growing. Her breathing was raspy, and her forehead was becoming crowded with beads of sweat. Her mother had warned her not to deal with advanced magic.

"It will only harm you," she had said. "You don't have the strength yet, you must wait, you must train, you must focus."

Well, nothing like the present. Gillian had been fourteen then. Her powers had begun to develop just a year before, when she had entered puberty. Well, three years should be enough. She didn't have to think about the other countless failed attempts and weakened mornings after her mother's death. Tonight, was different; it would work.

Gillian's hands tightened against the stuffed bear as she caught a faint flash of light, her ponytailed hair stinging her face as it continued moving, her lifeforce continuing to test its limits.

It's working!

She could feel the cool night air blowing against her now sticky skin, but it could do nothing to calm her struggles for gulps of air. She could feel her blood pressure rising, the strength of her lifeforce still pushing, but waning, her body looking for extra sources of energy.

Come out, mother! You know what this does to me!

Gillian knew her fatigue had gotten the better of her when she started coughing. She knew her lungs were struggling for air. She started to feel the dreadful sensation of drowning. The dizziness, the headache . . . but she was so close!

"Gillian Anne Cassidy, answer me!" Gillian gasped as she heard Addie's voice. What was the vampire doing at her house this early?

Suddenly, the attic plunged into darkness, the wind came to a stop, the candles blew out, and the quietness that spelled another failure settled in. All she could hear was her own ragged breath; all she could feel was the bear's soft embroidery against her cold and clammy skin.

Crap.

What time was it anyway? Maybe Addie wouldn't be too upset. She let out a hollow laugh. She wasn't thirteen anymore. She should stop caring so much about what Addie thought. That had been solely for her mother's benefit, so she could see that she cared about her friend.

But if she had done a better job with persuasion, her mom would've stayed and taken care of her. Maybe her mother would have accepted the offer of immortality. Instead of leaving her all alone, with a vampire prone to temper tantrums as a guardian. And, just like right now, refusing to come to her when she was needed.

Gillian felt a lone tear stinging her cheek. She tried to take a deep breath, but the coughing was still wreaking havoc on her lungs. She didn't have time for this. She had to recover. She would be able to communicate with her mother eventually, hopefully sooner rather than later. Hopefully before she got sick from spending too much of her lifeforce on a single spell that she couldn't seem to get right.

"You better not be in that attic. You promised you wouldn't, Gillian!" She could hear Addie climbing the steps.

8

Calm down, calm down. Show Addie you can do this.

But she could feel her strength draining. She had better make it back to her room before she couldn't stand on her feet.

"Damn it, Gillian! I know you're in there. Open the door or I swear I'll break it down."

She would have to, because Gillian had a feeling she wouldn't be able to get up for a while. Right now, all she could do was stare helplessly at the full moon peeking through the sole opened attic window on a tranquil spring night in Erie, Pennsylvania.

A full moon. That meant Dr. Wolfe would be changing into a lycan in just a little while. Wasn't Addie supposed to be with him, make sure nothing got out of hand? Addie had her own job to do—she needed to start trusting Gillian enough to leave her alone in her own house. Or soon to be, anyway. Sometimes, Gillian thought, Addie took the legal guardian thing too far. She was seventeen anyway, practically an adult. And since she couldn't convince her mom to live so she could finish her mother-rearing duties, what made Addie think she would do a better job anyway? She was an unmarried, childless, short-tempered immortal. What did she know about 2009 teenagers? Had she even been a teenager? The vampire couldn't even stand her own mother! Or so she had heard when she had been listening in on one of her mother's conversations with Addie. She knew she wasn't supposed to, but maybe she wouldn't have if her mother paid at least half the attention to her than she paid to Adelaide Brystol.

Gillian could hear Addie huff as she opened the attic door. After Addie broke it down several times,

Gillian just didn't bother to lock it anymore. After all, she was running out of excuses for the repairman. Short of "the vampire has more strength that she knows what do with, so you better take care not to get on her nerves," Gillian had tried everything. And she had bigger things to worry about. She was feeling weak now, but one thing was for sure. Addie would never deter her. And she would get her mother to come from wherever she was. Sooner or later.

"Gillian! Shit! Not again."

Gillian felt Addie's cold hands on her skin before it all went black.

Chapter 2

2008

Sixteen-year-old Gillian giggled as she tried to disentangle herself from Sean Kennard's lips.

"I told you, I have to go," she said as her palms settled on his shouldesrs, putting distance between herself and her brown-haired hunk of a boyfriend.

"But we just got out. And the sun's shining! How often do we get that in March? Come on, we can go to our favorite spot, so I can hold on to you for a few more moments." Sean winked at her, interlacing his warm fingers with hers.

"I told you I can't, Sean. I have to be somewhere."

"Your mom won't notice you being a few minutes late. She's probably sleeping anyway." He insisted on pulling her towards the back of the school building.

Gillian sighed. Sean was probably right. Since her diagnosis, her mother had been getting weaker by

the day; she couldn't pretend she was fine anymore
She could tell her mother struggled to keep her blue
eyes opened when Gillian visited. And her skin was
getting yellow. It was obvious that the anti-viral
medication had not worked. And as for a liver transplant, well, she was running out of time. She had to
do something. And where was Addie? Still recovering
from her shrapnel wounds. Or so Forrest had told the
hospital, and the army. She knew better. Addie was
still adjusting to her immortality. And phone calls
had not been enough to convince Gillian's mother to
accept immortality. No, Gillian had to take matters
into her own hands. And going to see Eric Callahan
was her first step.

"No. I'm going to see someone who can help her,
a friend of Addie's."

"Another doctor? Come on Gillian, we both
know—"

"This is different, Sean. This will help her. I'm sure
of it. But I gotta go now."

"Fine then, let me come with," Sean suggested, still
not relinquishing her hand.

"Can't. Got to go alone, his orders."

"His orders? Who is this guy? I won't let you go by
yourself. I will give him a piece of my mind if he so
much as looks at you the wrong way—"

"Sean," Gillian sighed. She really didn't have time
for his insecure temper flare-ups today. "It's for my
mom, I promise you, nothing more. Now can you
please let go? I'm late."

She could tell her boyfriend was struggling with
the request. But she didn't have time to assure him
anymore. Three months should have been enough to

assure him he was the only guy for her. What else did he want?

"Fine. But I'll call you later. And there better be no funny business."

"There won't be, I promise." She tiptoed, touching her lips to his in a quick kiss before taking off running from the schoolyard. "Talk to you later!"

"I'll hold you to it!"

She waved as she heard his voice while crossing the street. The street's honking cars would drown out her voice soon anyway. And she had to get to the park, sooner rather than later. Her mother's life depended on it. And skipping the bus meant she better quicken her pace.

Chapter 3

"Make me a vampire." Gillian gave Corporal Eric Callahan what she hoped was a confident smile.

A photo of Addie's platoon, sent by Addie to Gillian's Mom with a *no worries* letter attached a few weeks after deployment, along with a Google search, had revealed Eric Alan Callahan, US Army, now a car mechanic on his small self-owned business car garage and on the Army Reserve, who lived a few miles from Erie High School. A military career day had given her an excuse to introduce herself, and a phone call had piqued his interest when she revealed her friendship with Addie and the inconsistencies on his stellar service record. Immortality trying to hide in plain sight was a hoot. When Gillian had learned what her mother and Forrest had done with Addie's records, if only for Gillian to conceal the secret along with her lycan friend, it had become only too easy to spot another immortal through the world wide web of public military records.

"Well, little lady, when you asked to talk to me, I admit this isn't what I had in mind." Eric smiled back, and Gillian couldn't help but gasp when his incisors made an appearance in Erie's cool afternoon's sunlight. For many people, vampires were associated with night, but through her own personal experience, Gillian had learned that was a myth. Vampires could go out in sunlight; it would just weaken them. But as Eric was an older vampire, he had better control of his strength than she would when he made her one. It would take a while for her to reach the level of strength Eric currently possessed.

"Well, Corporal Callahan, that's what I want," Gillian said, trying to stop her voice from trembling and hoping the vampire wouldn't notice.

Yes, this was a big step. But it had to be done. She wanted to be there for her mother. If her mother wouldn't accept an offer to live forever from Addie, her best friend and mentee, she would surely accept it from her own daughter, right? She would have to. Gillian would make her see reason. That's all there was to it. Maybe it would hurt, but what was a little pain for the chance to live forever? What was a little unpleasantness for the chance to save her mother?

With her mother being on the verge of death, Gillian had learned the hard way, very fast, to appreciate what her mother was and had done for her. Her father, Martin Cassidy, had been declared MIA about six months after he was deployed to Afghanistan. Three years later, there was still no trace of him. It had taken both of them a while to accept that he was not coming back from Afghanistan, at least on the surface. Privately they believed there was still hope. Now all they had was each other, and Gillian wasn't going to throw that away. Or let her mother do it. If Addie wasn't going to get it done, she sure would.

"We can discuss payment arrangements. . . ," she continued. One more thing about immortality; it didn't come cheap. Allowance plus a part time job as a Shell gas station cashier on the weekends meant she had some money stashed up. After this payment plan, not much, if any, would be left.

"Whoa, hold up. We're not even near those details yet."

"But I—"

"Take it easy. We'll get there. But I have to ask, what's in it for you?"

Gillian took a deep breath. She hoped she wasn't sounding as annoyed as she felt.

Couldn't they just get it over with? Hepatitis B was an unforgiving and relentless disease, according to her earlier biology studies. And her mother's frail body was showing signs of shutting down, despite the doctors' best efforts. Her mother's clock was ticking. She needed help. Now.

"What's in it for me? I get to be immortal! Is there a bigger reason? Is there a bigger point? I'm a paying customer and I want—"

"Shut up. Just letting you know that once we do this, there's no turning back. So generally, I find that to make this choice, there's got to be a better reason than your *feelings of grandeur*. It won't do well for my reputation to have you finding ways to get rid of your immortality in a few years because you don't have what it takes. So, I would advise you, think carefully on this one, Miss Cassidy."

Eric's closeness was starting to make Gillian's skin crawl. Corporal Callahan was about thirty years her senior, or at least that is what he looked like in his immortal years. His blue eyes, short dark brown hair and rugged soldier face stayed youthful, if only with a few wrinkles around the eyes, but there was nothing young or kind in his cold stare. Considering his immortal strength and training, she had better be nice to him. That is, if she ever wanted to see her mother again.

Gillian let out a heavy sigh as she felt the floor begin to sway from under her feet. Her father wasn't coming back. And her mother, whose magic could surely be used to kick Eric where it hurt, was dying in a hospital bed. Her mother's best friend, who had immortality and could put it to good use, was seemingly content to let her mentor—the person responsible for sending her to medical school after orchestrating a lifesaving mission to make sure she survived her deployment in Afghanistan—die a painful death. Damn Addie!

"I don't want to lose anyone else I love. I won't have it. Not if there's a way around it. I won't lose… her," Gillian whispered, a lone tear escaping her left eye.

"Her?" Eric raised an eyebrow, crossing his arms.

Gillian hastily wiped away the rest of her tears.

"How is that your business?" Her voice suddenly carried her anger—the anger she couldn't express for fear of a bite gone wrong. She couldn't help anyone if she was dead. She would take care of Eric once she got what she needed. "I want immortality! Am I going to get it or not? And before you respond, you should know I'm a witch and can make your life very difficult if I don't get my way," Gillian said quietly, but clearly.

She hoped her voice sounded threatening. After all, could she really take him on? She wanted to believe that. But she was barely sixteen and had only touched the surface of her powers. In the end, she really hoped she was fooling him. Because there was no way she was fooling herself.

The sign he gave her wasn't reassuring her of her own pretend confidence, as the vampire merely scoffed. "Magic? Really? I can rip your throat out, little lady, before you can say *boo*." Gillian didn't think it was possible for Eric to get any closer, but it seemed she was mistaken. She stared into his misty blue eyes.

She should have quieted down. She should have run away. It seemed that this time, judging by the misty quality of his eyes, the vampire's temper might get the better of him. And she would make the perfect punching bag. She should have been scared. But the fate of her mother still lingered in the back of her mind.

"Please," she whispered, a sob escaping before she could help it. How long could she keep this up? Her mother was jaundicing at the hospital as they spoke!

"Now that's more like it," Eric whispered back, taking the liberty to stroke the honey-blond hair sitting on her shoulder.

Gillian turned her head, but she found she couldn't move. And she couldn't help the shakes that continued to escape her. But she could, would get through it. Immortality was just a means to an end, a remedy at a time when there was no other. She only had to stand Eric's presence a little bit more. She would take a long shower later.

"I'll find you soon, Gillian Anne," Eric whispered again, his cold breath, or what was left of it, in her ear.

"What do you mean? You'll give me what I want." Gillian finally found her voice, managing to back away from him.

"I'm giving you a chance to clear your shit up. I'll have to kill you, at least nearly, and that won't feel pleasant. Trust me. And it will make your friends wonder. So, make sure you use this time to cover your tracks, 'cause I will end you in every sense of the word if this in any way gets back to me." Eric Callahan put his hands in his light jacket's pockets and walked away as quietly as he had arrived.

Gillian released a breath she didn't know she was holding.

I can do this.

Chapter 4

2013

Gillian cursed as she opened her eyes to the ringing of her landline. She should've known better than to hope for the chance to sleep in. Not that she had been sleeping well to begin with.

"Hello?" She cleared her throat as she realized how raspy her voice sounded.

"I need you, Gill. How fast can you get to the hospital?"

"Addie, what's the matter?" Why would a surgeon call a med tech on her day off?

"It's Forrest." Gillian could feel Addie pause. Since when was Addie the type to choose words carefully?

"What about him?"

"He fainted."

"What?"

Being a lycan, Dr. Forrest Wolfe thought about bloody, medium-rare meat more than anything else.

She doubted that he of all people would suffer from low blood sugar.

"I bit him, and he fainted. Can you get here?" That was why Addie was choosing her words carefully. She was embarrassed.

Gillian didn't know Forrest's condition, but whatever it was, it would be exacerbated by the fact that the moon would be full tonight.

"I'll be right there."

Darting out of bed, Gillian grabbed the first pair of sweats she could find and a baby blue hoodie out of her dark wooden chest. Even if the day had promised to be sunny and warm in yesterday's evening news, her sketchy sleeping patterns would make for a cold morning anyway.

"Crap." Gillian caught her reflection in the bathroom mirror and picked up her hairbrush. Going on for a week now, the nightmares were taking their toll. Judging by the bags under her eyes and the greasy look of her light blond hair, her lack of sleep would be noticed by someone other than herself and her white and gray feline. Nevertheless, she had no time to analyze what the latest dream had meant or what the hell her ex had been doing in it . . . again.

She huffed as she threw the brush against the delicate crystal vanity table and scrunched her hair into a messy bun. Putting it off wouldn't help. It hadn't so far. Still, at the moment, Dr. Wolfe needed her more than she needed to sort her thoughts.

Gillian got her purse and caught sight of the beautiful woman smiling at her from the photograph on the living room coffee table.

"I miss you," she whispered.

Her glance drifted through her small kitchen and the remnants of yesterday's less-than-perfect potion mixes. They stared at her like a constant reminder that trying wasn't synonymous with a job well done.

"Yeah, thanks a lot, Mom. It's not like you offered to stay around and help, did you? Nope, you were perfectly fine leaving a sixteen-year-old on her own with an unpredictable vampire, whose ass I'm now running to save . . . again. Fantastic parenting job, I've got to tell you."

Later, she would regret insulting the memory of the dead. But that would have to wait until she took care of the undead, and her associated immortal friend.

❖

"I'm so sorry," Gillian apologized as she collided with a third nurse in less than fifteen minutes. A busy hospital and her lack of sleep were proving to be a particularly bad combination. Unlike the other two, this nurse didn't stop to acknowledge her apology.

"Ignore her. Jeannie always has a bad day," Addie dismissed it. "Are you all right? Did you get enough sleep?"

"Some. Anyway, where's Dr. Wolfe? Whoa! Crazy day, huh?" Gillian dodged a gurney.

"School bus accident, part of the reason I had to work a double shift again. Right there." Addie pointed to a wooden door between the offices of the general surgeons.

"A janitor's closet? Couldn't you at least have put him in a patient's room?"

"What, and risk getting fired if a patient suddenly passes by and sees you in action? I'm having enough trouble with the sunlight as it is. Besides, it wasn't my fault! I didn't have time to look for blood before—"

"Here," Gillian slipped the pint out of her purse. "You look like you need it."

And she did. Even though she had supposedly fed from the werewolf, Addie still looked a tinge paler than usual. Her black, shoulder-length, ponytailed hair was matted, and her green eyes were lighter than they would have been had she fed properly. She almost looked a little light-headed. Of course, Gillian couldn't imagine werewolf blood being half as nutritious as the supply coming from people whose systems weren't compromised by a virus. And working a double shift, including the graveyard one, couldn't have helped.

Gillian smiled as Addie took out her hunter green coffee mug from her bag. She always thought it was neat how it matched her friend's beautiful green eyes. She suddenly felt very self-conscious about her sweatpants, greasy hair, and baggy-eyed appearance. Next to a vampire, engineered to look attractive, she must look very plain. That she imagined Addie had always been attractive, even in her non-vampire years, was beside the point. When she was granted immortality in Afghanistan, Addie had been a twenty-five-year-old nurse who was trying to make it to medical school. Her immortality had taken care to preserve her youthful, elegant, if paler skin and her straight, jet-black hair. She had never taken to makeup, despite her mother's best efforts, but there was a trace of glamour and confidence in her hard-to-read, classically beautiful face.

Not that Gillian hadn't had her share of suitors. She had inherited her mother's blond hair that curled at the ends, and her father's light brown eyes. But immortality wouldn't have been so attractive, once upon a time, if it didn't have its perks. And those perks included a predatory magnetism that mortals couldn't tear their eyes away from.

"You all right?" Addie asked, taking a long sip out of her mug.

"Yeah, no worries," Gillian answered.

With the look Addie was giving her, Gillian could tell her friend wouldn't have left well enough alone if they hadn't reached their destination. Damn, how she wished Addie could direct her observations and conclusions somewhere else once in a while.

Gillian gasped as the sight before her eyes made her forget about her own conundrums. She didn't know what she was expecting, but to say that the werewolf had looked better was an understatement. His dark blond hair was disheveled, his forehead heavy with perspiration, and the white T-shirt he wore under a red sweater was stained with blood along the neckline. Although he wasn't conscious, she could tell his body was fighting the vampire trace.

"I'm sorry . . ." Addie started to apologize, just like Gillian knew she would.

"Shhh. No worries, he'll be fine in no time. But I'll have to zoom him with me." What was done was done. Now they had to fix it.

Addie nodded.

In a matter of seconds, Gillian had Forrest up by one arm, Addie holding the other. *Thank God for vampire strength.* "We'll be at my place."

"I'll be there after chart duty."

24

Gillian couldn't help but chuckle. If there was something every physician hated, it was paperwork. "Fine. Do you need some more?" The vampire did look better after drinking her fill from the green mug.

"Not now. I'll be by later," Addie assured her. "Can you take care of him on your own?"

"Yeah. Do what you need to do."

A little concentration should do it.

"Damn it," Addie cursed, and Gillian felt her drop her share of the werewolf's weight. Gillian couldn't help but stumble under his body. "Sorry." Addie quickly took hold of Forrest once again, eyes on her beeper.

"What's the matter?" Gillian asked. She should have been annoyed. After all, Forrest needed attention, and she desperately needed coffee, but she figured Addie had been through enough today. Forrest was immortal; he would be fine.

"Make that a lot later. Winston wants to see me."

Gillian chuckled. She could tell her friend would be dragging her feet to the chief of surgery's office.

"What does he want?" Gillian knew she should be making less conversation and focusing on Forrest. But this conversation would hopefully calm Addie down.

"We'll see."

"All right. I'll keep it warm for you."

"Thanks, Gillian. I'm so sorry to bother you on your day off."

"No worries. See you later. Dr. Wolfe will be fine, you know that, right?"

Addie sighed as she passed her hand through her now shiny black hair. *She's nervous.* Gillian couldn't blame her.

"Yeah. I'm so sorry, he just..."

"It's okay. We'll talk about it later."

Gillian was afraid that if Addie kept talking about it, the vampire might actually tear up. Now that her appetite was gone, Addie was calmer and could think more clearly. Even as a vampire, the graveyard shift was not the best mood settler, especially as a double shift, not to mention the guilt she was probably feeling. Yep, later would be better. She would take care of Dr. Wolfe first. Although she couldn't help but wonder what exactly had led Addie to bite him. Was there something between them? Fooling around that got out of hand?

As soon as she realized what she was thinking and where it was leading, Gillian shrugged it off. She had no time to ponder that particular subject. Besides, it was none of her business. Why should she care what Addie and Forrest did behind closed doors? They had known each other long enough.

Sighing, she prepared for the dizziness that would follow her choice of transportation. With her powers still developing and training from a grimoire instead of a flesh and blood witch, as she should have been doing, it would take a lot of concentration to zoom two people. She had done it before, but the second person was usually conscious. Damn, she should have made coffee before she went to sleep last night. With Dr. Wolfe's weight, there was no way she would be able to make a pit stop at Starbucks on her way home.

Chapter 5

Gillian yelped as both she and Forrest landed on her baby-blue, quilted bed, scaring her cat off her pillow in the process.

"Sorry, Dagonet!" Gillian apologized to her companion. Dagonet had been her mother's kitten, the last cat she had brought home before she succumbed to Hepatitis B because of an accidental needle stab.

The cat was unimpressed. He meowed in protest and jumped off the bed, an intent *I'll get you later* look in his blue-green eyes while he made his way lazily to her bathroom.

After resolving to make it up to Dagonet later, Gillian sighed in relief. Other than landing on top of the werewolf, there had been no damage done. Furniture had been broken, along with bones, when she was just learning to master this power in her teenage years. It was nice, for once, to see a glimmer of improvement.

With a grunt, she got off the bed. If she didn't know any better, she would say that the werewolf was comfortable. But noticing that the amount of perspiration had increased on his forehead, she extended her hand to check his temperature.

She gasped. His forehead was so hot she was surprised he was still breathing. *He's immortal,* she reminded herself. That was probably the only reason he was still here. She had felt heat as she had landed but was accustomed to the fact that men did tend to conserve more body heat than women.

Gillian willed her mind to focus on the spicy cinnamon smell that lived in her room, her eyes fixed on the bears that occupied the table next to her bedside window. The smell came from an enchanted candle that she would never get rid of. It had been a present from her mother when she had begun to practice her powers. Bridget had always told her that she needed something to focus on when her mind became too overwhelmed. She had used cinnamon, and crochet. Gillian hadn't appreciated arts and crafts when she was thirteen and just beginning to learn the art of witchcraft.

Death could certainly do a lot to change someone's mind.

She cleared her throat, willing the tears to stay in their place for the evening. She had to focus on Dr. Wolfe right now. She knew why this was happening: his lycan virus was fighting Addie's trace in his blood. There was no magic fix for this that she knew of. The best she could do was to give him a sedative, Valium being probably the first choice. The tranquilizer would force his muscles to relax, his blood flow to slow down, and maybe, the perspiration would slowly stop. It was worth a shot. There was only one problem: a sedative would prevent Forrest from fighting and expelling the vampire trace left by Addie's bite. He would have to be conscious for that, or so she had read in her mother's grimoire. Thanks to friends like Addie, Bridget had made sure to add a section on vampires to her magical fountain of knowledge and had made sure to write it down so Gillian could continue with the association and care of her immortal friend. Unfortunately, she would never know where her mother had gotten that knowledge. There were other witches, other grimoires that theoretically a witch could get her hands on if she knew where to look. But supernatural beings, both the immortal and those with an expiration date attached, were saddled with their own issues. And they rarely traveled in packs. Of these, werewolves would be the most family oriented, as a lycan could be both born and made. But Gillian had yet to meet Dr. Wolfe's family; a strong sign that supernatural beings didn't easily trust each other. Hell, she was sure that Forrest and Addie wouldn't even be friends if Forrest hadn't done that favor for her mother . . . or maybe they would. Had they been fooling around today? Well, there was only one way to find out.

But first things first: she really didn't have the luxury of waiting around for his body to take care of its current predicament on its own, assuming he would be able to. Granted, he was immortal, but from a different species. And she really didn't want him to be the test case for some reaction that she didn't know how to deal with.

Trying to gather her concentration against the werewolf's groans, Gillian conjured an injection full of the sedative. She heaved a sigh of relief as it appeared in her hand. Usually, when she couldn't completely focus, her magic just wouldn't work. Maybe, just maybe, today was her lucky day.

Once again, she got close to the werewolf and felt his forehead. If it were possible, the back of her hand felt hotter than when she had first gotten out of bed.

Now where would Addie have bitten you? She figured it would be best if the tranquilizer went that same route. If, as she had thought at first, they had been fooling around, Addie would have gone for the jugular.

Gillian approached the bed, her baby-blue quilt now drenched with sweat, and pushed Forrest's dark blond hair back. She briefly marveled at how soft it felt, despite its dampness.

He groaned, the perspiration again thick in his sandy eyebrows. She let out a deep breath. There was a reason she had not elected to be a nurse; she was afraid something would go wrong, either with her or with her patients. After all, her mother had pretty much been a victim of her profession. She had gotten hep B from an accidental needle poke and the doctors hadn't been able to manage the virus or get her a liver transplant in time.

"Damn it!" She took hold of the wooden bed canopy, trying to calm herself down. Closing her eyes, she inhaled the comforting cinnamon scent once more. Her palm on Forrest's wet neck, she inserted the needle swiftly. The werewolf's groan told her he was still in pain.

"Not for much longer." That was what she hoped, anyway.

Sighing, she sat down at the corner of the bed, hesitantly putting her hand on his head.

"I wonder . . ." Gillian began massaging Forrest's scalp. The motion had always calmed her down when her mother had done it to her.

Slowly, but perceptibly, Forrest's breaths began to slow down. Hopefully, that meant he was starting to feel better. Gillian allowed herself to relax into the bed, her eyes closing as she leaned against the header. Now that the adrenaline had stopped pumping, she was feeling last night's sleeplessness catching up with her. Where was that coffee?

"Gillian."

Gillian's eyes shot open.

Forrest's eyes were still closed. Had she dreamt that? She was sure she hadn't drifted asleep. How could he—how did he know she was there?

Of course, he would know. He was a werewolf. He would always recognize her scent. Nevertheless, she got out of bed. Now that he was more relaxed, she supposed he didn't need her anymore.

And she desperately needed coffee, and a shower.

❖

Gillian smiled as she combed her hair in front of the steamed mirror, inhaling her shampoo's coconut scent. A long bath had been just what the doctor ordered. Granted, she was starving, but after that hectic morning, appetite had been the last thing on her mind.

Putting her fluffy, baby-blue terry bathrobe on, she pressed her ear to the door that led to her bedroom. She figured no noise meant that the werewolf was still sleeping. With the vampire trace undoubtedly trying to wreak havoc on his own lycan virus, she couldn't blame him. If his body was still fighting the effects of this morning's "accident," he probably would be sleeping well after nightfall, which is when his body would begin the lycan transformation. It was going to be a full moon, and a long night. She better put a pot of coffee on before getting that dinner . . .

Gillian opened the door to her bedroom and gasped. Forrest Wolfe was standing up and staring in her direction, looking dazed. She suddenly became very aware of the fact she was wearing only a robe. She figured that he noticed as well, because he refused to look her in the eyes and she could see his cheeks turning crimson.

"Um, hi?" Forrest whispered. "Sorry, I didn't—"

"Excuse me a minute, Dr. Wolfe." Gillian picked up jeans and a T-shirt from her closet and went back to the bathroom.

"I gather you're feeling better?" Her inquiry sounded kind of silly since he was up, but she saw no other way to start the conversation.

"Yes. Thank you, Gillian," he said, smiling.

"No problem."

How to approach this? Oh, how she wished Addie were here. The werewolf, it seemed, sensed her hesitation.

"Something wrong? I really do feel better."

"Yes, I'm glad. But it won't last through the night. Not unless I keep you sedated. And that would—"

"Would what? What's going on, Gillian?"

"You ever been bitten by a vampire, Dr. Wolfe?" she finally asked him. There was no other way to bring it up. Why would he allow Addie to do it without discussing the consequences? There was only one possible answer in her mind.

"Um, no."

She looked at him directly. She briefly marveled at the fact that even though his clothes were rumpled and his hair untidy, he still looked cute. She attributed it to never seeing him outside his very neat work clothes and scrubs. "Immortal or not, your body is fighting a virus."

"I know, Gill."

"No, Dr. Wolfe, not *your* virus, the vampire trace. If you were a mortal, you would be dead, understand?"

"Okay, but I'm not, so it's fine."

"You're not because your lycan virus is fighting the vampire trace. You're immortal. Don't you immortals keep track of what other species could do to you?" She approached him and touched the back of her hand to his forehead. He flinched, just slightly. "Still burning," she whispered, more to herself than to him. "You'll only get hotter as the full moon approaches."

"What do you mean? And to answer your question, no, we rarely if ever partake in an inter-species relationship, so there's no need. The only way to keep off each other's throats and not cause a scene in a world full of mortals is to keep our distance."

"Well, you should, just, you know . . . you never know." Gillian shrugged. This arrangement sounded more like Cold War Détente diplomacy than anything else, a bomb ready to explode if even a hair

33

was touched the wrong way. But she wasn't about to make that her business; she didn't have time at the moment. But where did Addie fit into this picture of species separation?

Gillian, focus.

"You're a doctor—think of it as an infection. The lycan virus is fighting to get the vampire trace out of your body, which means your body right now is weakened. It's still going to try to transform though. You're in for a rough night. I could give you another sedative to prevent the transformation from happening and make you more comfortable. Goodness, I certainly thought that Valium would last longer. If you were mortal, it would have. Anyway, I could sedate you, but . . ."

"Yeah?"

"It would mean that your body wouldn't be able to get rid of Addie's trace completely. In order for it to make its way out of your body, your own virus needs to be actively fighting it. It won't do that if sedation is fighting for attention."

Gillian reached for her pink sweater from her dresser. She couldn't shake the unnerving feeling that this topic was bringing to her body. But why? It shouldn't have come as a surprise that Addie and Forrest would eventually, maybe, be more than friends.

"And what would that mean?" Forrest's question successfully distracted her from that uncomfortable train of thought.

"Theoretically, according to my mother's grimoire anyway . . . her magic book," she added as she caught his lost gaze. She supposed the interspecies separation applied to witches as well. "As I've never seen this myself, you would crave blood every so often. It'd probably make you stronger. I doubt the sunlight would affect you, and maybe when Addie bites you again the consequences against your body won't be so noticeable."

"All right, so no sedative."

His answer surprised her. Wouldn't he want that if they were moving the relationship to the next stage? Gillian shook her head. She didn't need that image. And her stomach was growling. It was well into the afternoon now. This no food in her stomach until the patient feels better was getting on her nerves.

"Fine. But if Addie bites you again, this may work against you."

"It won't happen again."

"No?" Gillian did her best to sound detached from this revelation.

"No, Gillian. She didn't want to do it in the first place. It was sort of an accident . . . well, not really." The werewolf refused to look her in the eye for the second time that day. "Didn't Addie tell you what happened?" This whole topic was making her stomach turn. She should've felt happy for her friends. Why wasn't that the case was a question to ponder.

"Kind of hard to find time, Dr. Wolfe. You were obviously in distress."

"Fair enough. And Gillian?"

"Mm?"

"Would it kill you to call me by my first name? We aren't at the hospital anymore, no need to be so formal. I mean, you did get me out of this mess."

Gillian decided she would not have this discussion again. She had used the formal title for his profession for as long as she had known him, no reason to stop now. It wasn't like they were the best of friends or anything. Besides, keeping him at a professional distance despite their long acquaintance made it easier for her to dismiss the less than professional thoughts that had been plaguing her of late. Anyway, she had to get something substantial in her stomach. And soon.

"Would you care for something to eat?"

Forrest cleared his throat before answering. "Sure."

The delay in his response let her know he was a tad annoyed at the change of subject. But she also knew him well enough to know that he was far too polite to bring it up again.

"Come on. I'll help you get downstairs."

His puzzled face was an expected reaction. After all, mortal men seldom admitted they needed help, what would make immortal ones any different? If anything, they'd be more appalled by the prospect. "Gillian, I appreciate it, but I'll be fine."

Case in point.

"You're in a severely weakened state, Dr. Wolfe. Let me help." Without waiting for his reply, she took his hand and led him slowly out of her bedroom and toward the stairs.

She felt him stumble while walking, probably because her gesture had taken him by surprise. But she was prepared for it. Gillian closed her eyes as her foot touched felt the cold surface of the first step.

"Uh, Gillian, I—"

She chuckled and briefly opened her eyes to see, with satisfaction, the lycan literally hovering next to her.

"Yes, I am aware you're afraid of heights, but it sure beats sustaining a wound when you're at your weakest. Now, close your eyes and mouth, and we'll be fine. It's just stairs."

"I am not! If Addie told you that, I'll have you know—"

"Forrest, please," Gillian whispered, effectively quieting him for the sole reason that she used his first name. It was nice to know that she still had her wit when great concentration for an optimum magical performance was required. Having accomplished said task, they slowly descended the stairs. She would make fun of him later.

In the process of quieting Addie's gray-eyed friend, Gillian had missed her furry cat, named after the *Legends of King Arthur and the Knights of the Round Table*. The tales had been one of her mother's favorite books. The feline, while climbing upstairs, probably felt threatened by the lycan close to the roof and hissed loudly. His protest interrupted Gillian's concentration. She stumbled slightly and stepped on the cat's tail, making the feline screech.

"Dag!" Gillian cursed as her focus broke and Forrest began an unexpected and unplanned descent into her and then towards the bottom of the stairs.

Chapter 6

Addie sighed as she opened the door to the break room, laptop in hand.

"Please let this be quick." Her whisper echoed into the empty room. She could think of a thousand different things she'd rather do than finish up her paperwork. Walking the twenty miles back to her place in Erie's cool air, or the ten miles back to Gillian's place, even in the messy April rain, unfed, sounded more appealing than sitting in the warm hospital with a stack of patient charts to complete.

"Addie?"

Addie looked up as she was taking a seat at a table, and she rolled her eyes as she caught sight of who it was.

"What do you want, Josh?" Her eyes didn't waver from her work. Right now, she wanted to finish it more than she wanted not to appear rude to her ex. That ship had already sailed. Why bother?

"I thought you were going out with Gillian today."

"Yes, well, Forrest had an accident, so Gillian is busy. Besides, I need to finish charts."

"Oh. Is he all right?" Josh asked.

Addie watched Dr. Josh Ambrose take his scrub cap off and pass his hand through his shiny and straight black hair. It had been that hair and those piercing blue eyes that contrasted with his paper-white skin and toned athletic body that had made her fall for him. If it wasn't for that temper of his . . .

"Nothing that Gillian can't take care of," she said. She knew he was only feigning concern. He was nice to her friends on occasion, but only for her sake.

"You left them by themselves?" He sounded amused.

"What am I, Forrest's keeper?" She went back to typing. Since Josh seemed to have nothing but small talk for her, there was no point in giving him her undivided attention. But his comment lingered in the back of her brain. What was wrong with leaving Forrest and Gillian by themselves?

"I was going for Gillian's keeper, really."

"Say what you have to say and get out, yes?" she said, cutting his statement short. Her charts still looked depressingly incomplete.

"Are you all right?"

Addie sighed once more, willing her patience to stay with her just a little bit longer. What would it take for him to leave her alone? She was trying really hard to be polite. "I'm just peachy, but behind on these." She lifted the laptop she was working on just in case he had missed it. After all, they had bonded on their profound abhorrence of paperwork once upon a time. "So, if you don't mind, I'd like to finish before long."

"You've fed."

Addie could detect slight surprise on his tone. She supposed her shiny hair and red lips were a dead giveaway. Still, she had to eat, so the surprise was just uncalled for.

"I had to. Or did you forget you fed off me this morning?" Addie looked up and was startled to find Josh right in front of her. The last time she had glanced at him he was barely inside the door. Well, vampires would be vampires.

"I didn't take much, so you shouldn't have been that weakened." Josh suddenly went silent, crossing his arms. "Addie, you never told me what kind of accident Wolfe was in."

Addie frowned. Josh never called Forrest by just his last name in front of her, usually because he wanted to remain in her good graces. Nope, only Gillian called him Dr. Wolfe, both in and outside the hospital. Addie couldn't figure out why after years of knowing him, Gillian still called Forrest a "friend by association."

Nevertheless, what had happened this morning remained none of Josh's business.

"I told you, nothing that Gillian couldn't take care of."

"Must have been pretty bad to have a witch come to the rescue."

Addie sighed, being careful to place her hands on the computer's mouse pad. Smashing the computer right now, no matter how good it would feel at the moment, would mean another write-up in her file, for being reckless, if a little accident prone, not to mention prone to temper flare-ups. There was also the fact that she had not saved her work yet. And she did not trust her computer to do it. Technology was nothing if not inconsistent. But this time, the surgeon did not bother to hide her annoyance. Josh apparently had something up his sleeve and was not letting it go. That meant that as long as he kept pestering her, she would get no work done.

"Josh, what's your point? Just say what you want to say."

"Did you feed off him?"

"What?" Whatever his problem was, she did not expect *that* to be it.

"You did, didn't you?"

Addie just shrugged. She wasn't in the mood for an argument. The two of them had fed that day; if their tempers got the better of them, there was a high probability someone would get hurt. And an incident like that wouldn't look good on a physician's file.

"Answer me! I can smell his stinking cologne on you." Josh moved around the table and took Addie by her shoulders. He pulled her up from her chair, which fell over.

"Would you get a hold of yourself?" Addie removed his hands. She had to pass her tongue over her fangs to keep them from coming out.

"What happened between Forrest and me is none of your business," she hissed, noticing that Josh's blue eyes were glistening. Their color had turned a misty liquid, and his fangs were barely concealed. Yep, tempers had officially flared. But he had started it.

"It is if he takes my girl's blood!" he bellowed.

LIFEFORCE

"I'm not your girl, Josh. Now get off!" Addie pushed him back, slamming him against the refrigerator.

"We came damn close!"

"It didn't happen! And if you hadn't fed from me this morning, *this* wouldn't have happened! Not that I have to justify my actions to you." She should learn to keep her voice down. She didn't want to be responsible for waking patients up with details they'd rather she kept to herself.

Yes, she shouldn't have let him feed off her, that was a big *no-no* as far as exes were concerned, as pheromones were always involved in the feeding. That was part of how the vampire fed, part of their predatory mechanisms. There was no way to fully control it.

But it had been a long night, and Gillian had the day off. Yes, there was a fridge solely reserved for them and she had a copy of Gillian's keys with her at all times. No other tech was allowed to enter, no one but those Gillian authorized. The hospital likely had just assumed that she was a very private person. She was nice otherwise, if a little quiet. But she got the job done. There was no need to ask questions, and Addie made sure to shut them down early if they came in.

And Addie had needed the distraction the pheromones would provide. Yes, even though immortality led to not feeling shocked by what she did in a day-to-day basis, saving lives was still plenty stressful on its own. And death was never taken well. Both surgeons had been tired, and disappointed. But she could not get off, her shift was not over, not yet.

But his had been. And he had been starving.

One thing had led to another in his then empty on-call room.

42

One mistake, never to happen again.

Not if she could help it.

Of course, she had not counted on an extended shift due to an emergency caused by that school bus crash.

And Forrest, he had stepped up when he didn't have to.

If she had not been so foolish, Forrest and Gillian wouldn't be in this situation.

It was over between Josh and her. So over.

"You're not pulling that one, Addie. Gillian always has you covered."

"Do *not* bring Gillian into this."

"She always has a supply of fresh blood! There was no need for you to seek it elsewhere." He crossed his arms again. "You made him want you, didn't you?"

The thought of actually having done that (and Addie hoped she hadn't, at least Forrest hadn't said anything) made her stomach mildly upset. Then again, Forrest was not an ugly man, not in the least. His blond hair and gray eyes along with the mildly tanned features of a man who liked physical activity around sunlight in an environment that was almost always overcast, had probably been the fantasy of more nurses and doctors than she cared to count, along with more than a few patients. After all, his good looks still dominated his youthful face, despite the fact that he had been born around the end of the First World War. She decided to use that little fact to her advantage. It promised to be, at this moment, enormously satisfying.

"Maybe I did. I was busy, so excuse me if I wasn't paying attention!"

"Shut up, *shut up*!"

They both quieted down and stared at the door as a nurse entered the room. Both vampires glared at her.

"Sorry, thought Dr. Ikes might be here," the light-blue-scrubbed lady muttered, closing the door quickly as she backed out. She had probably been looking for one of them. During their relationship the hospital had been privy to many loud arguments. By now, nurses, and anybody else for that matter, knew better than to interrupt. Regardless, the nurse had provided an excellent stopping point. Addie started to the exit. She needed to handle the nurse. If she had been eavesdropping, she had to shut down questions. Although she doubted that any nurse would give her trouble. She had a reputation of being efficient, and in possession of a volatile temper. By now, her colleagues should have known better than to inquire about something personal. But just to make sure . . .

"We're not done." Josh grabbed her arm before she could take two steps.

Addie decided to take the more direct approach. She clasped her right hand around Josh's neck, and in one second, he was practically pasted against the wall.

"We were done before you decided my private affairs were your concern," she growled.

"You do know why you're so strong right now, don't you, Addie?" he whispered.

Addie chuckled. "Honestly, Josh, I couldn't care less. It sure feels great from where I'm standing." On any other occasion she would have been puzzled by her suddenly dominating grip, especially because Josh was the older vampire and, therefore, that much stronger than her.

He continued. "The lycan's strength is still in your body. Well, enjoy it while it lasts. Of course, one can't be sure of the repercussions of such an event."

"Save your fake worries, Josh. You should know by now that I don't respond well to threats." She gripped tighter at his neck.

"Oh no, Addie, not you. I meant the aftereffects of your feeding on the blood provider."

Addie dropped her ex against the opposite wall before he could finish his statement. Knowing how vain he was and how he had always been the jealous type, she should have expected this tantrum.

"Sleep it off, Josh. Or find somebody to sleep it off with, whatever works for you."

"There was never anyone but y—"

"But mess with Forrest, and he will be the least of your problems." Forrest was her friend. And she didn't need to justify that to anyone, much less Josh. She took her bag and quietly left the break room.

Chapter 7

Gillian moaned as she tried to get used to her surroundings from her position on the cold, gray-tiled floor. It was only made slightly warmer by the werewolf cushioning her.

When this had been her family's house, her mother had done everything to make it feel like a home. Her father had purchased it when he had enlisted, and her mother had done everything possible to keep Gillian from focusing on his absence once he was deployed. The house had been warmed by beige curtains, brown-carpeted floors, sunshine-yellow bathroom tiles, and, of course, crocheted teddy bears in each one of the three cozy bedrooms.

When her father went missing in Afghanistan, her mother did everything she could to keep up the warmth and comfort, a homage to the way things had been. The only difference being that she had added a coffin to the basement when she had orchestrated Addie's survival and return from her medical unit in Afghanistan. Coffins were the only thing that allowed a vampire to sleep well, because the darkness signaled to the body to stay still. With death, circadian rhythm as well as blood flow went out the window, so energy was not well distributed without a quiet, dark place to replenish. The basement as a location also helped, as it minimized the noises from the main level. Thank goodness her mother had kept the house instead of buying an apartment. But of course, she was the one that had insisted that Addie live forever, so she knew what she was doing.

But Gillian's mother's death and Addie's subsequent temporary move-in and guardianship had been hard on Gillian and Addie both. And once Gillian turned eighteen and the house deed was passed to her, she didn't want anything in it that reminded her of the home she used to share with her mother. A mother that had chosen a painful death over infinite time with her daughter, the proper time to love her and continue teaching her the powers she was sucking at right about now.

And so, the carpeted floors had been restored to their original tiled surface. Sparse decoration, mostly the few keepsakes that Gillian couldn't part with and purple curtains, made for a spartan and uncluttered, if cold, home. Finally, the basement's space had been reduced further by the addition of a werewolf cage in a separate room across from the coffin. All she had left to do was get rid of the old house paint cans.

Although a born lycan, Forrest's ferocity when a full moon appeared was nothing to be trifled with. It was difficult to control a lycan's wolf-like instincts to feed on live prey. No doubt Forrest's experience had helped him with the control issues, not to mention the fact that Addie had asked Gillian to tone down his rage magically. Now his transformation took more time, and his strength was not as fierce, his emotions not truly overtaken by his instincts. She was quite proud of that, and he was grateful, although he had never explained the reason behind this request even though Addie had told her it had come from him. Speaking of the basement, that was where Forrest should be just now. Why were they still on the floor?

"Wow, sorry, this is really embarrassing," Gillian whispered.

"Don't worry about it. Are you okay?" Forrest was sprawled next to her on the floor, having rolled from beneath her. He exhaled and his breath against her ear made her shiver. And also realize that if her supine arm by his forehead was any indication, he was burning more by the minute.

"I'm fine." Gillian put her hands against the floor to hoist herself up, wincing as she felt a sharp pain shoot through her ankle.

"Gillian?"

"I'm fine!" This was not the time to get sidetracked. She had to get him fed and caged in the basement soon. "Let's get you some dinner. You should eat before sunset." She started walking into the kitchen, trying hard not to limp.

"I'll get it." He gently pushed Gillian toward a stool and grabbed a steak out of the fridge, the black one labeled "food," before sitting down. Gillian always kept fresh meat in there for him, right beside Addie's white fridge, labeled "Addie." She knew that tired physicians could get distracted, so labels prevented confusion, and gagging.

"How long have you and Addie been friends, Gillian?"

Strange question. Gillian cleared her throat. She got up and headed to the fridge herself. That way she wouldn't have to watch Forrest eat his rare meat. "A long time, Dr. Wolfe."

"So, you knew Addie when she and your mom were friends?"

Gillian shook her head. "Not really. Mom was Addie's friend way before I was. I didn't keep tabs on my mother's friends at work. I hated tagging along when she had to go to the hospital for whatever reason. It'd be different now, I guess."

"You were sixteen, Gillian, and you couldn't have known that you would have only a limited amount of time left with her."

"What's this about, Dr. Wolfe?" Gillian wasn't about to unload her emotional baggage.

"I was just wondering how you knew so much about the effects of vampire bites."

"I read a lot and Addie has clarified a few things, being a vampire and a doctor after all. Being her blood supplier has entitled me to ask a lot of questions that Mom must have clarified for her in her plan for her to be immortal. Of course, in my mom's mind, I was still too young to understand—such bullshit, excuse my French. So, she left in her grimoire whatever she felt she couldn't explain in person. How's the rib eye?" She smiled as she noticed his empty plate. "You should get to your cage. The vampire trace will fight your transformation tonight, so you'll be safer here than at your apartment. Plus, I'll need to keep an eye on you since we don't know how your body will react. No need to wait for me, you have a long night ahead of you."

"Oh, come on, Gillian, the least I can do is keep you company."

"Addie will be here soon anyway."

"Gillian—"

"Trust me, Dr. Wolfe. It's for your own good." She could still see his reluctance as he cleared his throat.

"Okay. Good night, then. And thanks." He headed towards the wooden door that would provide access down to the basement.

"Sure," Gillian said as she watched him disappear down the stairs.

"Damn it," she cursed as she sat down. Now her ankle was really bothering her. She'd need a pain reliever and an anti-inflammatory medication before going to bed.

"Are you all right?"

Gillian gasped. Addie was standing by the kitchen doorway. How long she'd been standing there was anyone's guess. Vampires could be pretty sneaky when they wanted to be.

"Yeah. Long day."

"Mm." Addie gave her that same look from this morning: worried with a trace of contempt, a sign that she really didn't believe exhaustion was all there was to it. Oh, how Gillian wished she could be a better liar. "Where's Forrest?"

"I just sent him down. I think his body's going to fight the transformation."

"Will he be able to go through it tonight? Weakened like that?"

"I doubt it. I'll keep an eye on him though."

"Is he going to be all right?" Addie motioned towards a chair. Gillian nodded. She couldn't believe that Addie still asked permission to sit down even though they had been friends for so long. Maybe Forrest's excessive politeness, for lack of a better term, had rubbed off on her.

"After tonight, yes. So I've read anyway. My mom's grimoire doesn't get much more specific than that," Gillian answered, shifting uncomfortably once more. Her ankle was getting to her. And her exhaustion was not helping matters.

Addie must have noticed. Nothing could get by her, not even when she had been a young nurse, or so Gillian's mother had said.

"You should start calling it your grimoire, don't you think? Bridget passed it on to you, didn't she?"

"You know I haven't fully mastered my powers yet."

Her book still had her mother's name printed in graceful calligraphy on the first page in spelled ink— ink that ensured it would never fade.

The grimoire had been passed down the Cassidy bloodline for generations, and every time a new witch mastered the powers and needed to replace a deceased one, the name would change, the owner would change, and the magical responsibility would shift. It was not Gillian's time yet. Her mother's death had been premature, to put it delicately.

"Gillian, is something—"

"What happened between you and Dr. Wolfe, Addie?" Gillian interjected. She really didn't want to get into why her ankle was throbbing. Falling because you let your cat break your magical concentration wasn't going to go over very well. It would make Addie inquire further about her sleeping patterns and she wasn't in the mood to discuss her nightmares.

Addie sighed. Gillian could tell she was not pleased by the avoidance of the question or by the uncomfortable topic. But Gillian figured she deserved an answer, especially when she had to go to the hospital on her day off to fix the mess. "It was an accident, Gillian. He shouldn't have offered to do it. He should've looked for my mug instead."

Gillian could tell that Addie was embarrassed. She was absolutely refusing to look at her. She was instead entertaining herself by looking inside her bag, no doubt for her blood mug.

"Well, you must have looked pretty drained. When was the last time you'd fed?"

"It wasn't my fault. That accident, I had to scrub in—"

"How long?"

"Twelve hours."

"Addie!" She was lucky she hadn't collapsed in the OR.

"It's work, Gillian. Patients aren't immortal."

No matter how much Gillian disapproved of Addie not taking care of herself, the vampire was right. As a doctor, Addie was responsible for the well-being of others. Her mother had been the exact same way. And her work had killed her.

Gillian let out a deep breath. If one thing was for sure, she wasn't in the mood for another one of those "meaning of life" pep talks. Her mother had been famous for those, especially when Gillian began mastering her powers shortly after she hit puberty. Now really, who can control their magical powers when they can barely control their emotions? Suffice it to say, being a thirteen-year-old witch was something that Gillian could have done without, even though she had to admit that having powers had felt pretty exciting at the time. But her youthful foolishness combined with her inability to control her powers fully had let to some foolish decisions. Ones she would take back if she could.

Right now, though, this wasn't about her. Right now, her curiosity was getting the better of her. Right now, she really wanted to know if something more than friendship was going on between Forrest and Addie. Why exactly? That was a question to ponder later.

"Fine. And what happened after that?"

"Forrest saw me and how weak I was, determined that I wasn't going to make it to my on-call room . . . I could have though," Addie said defensively. "He pulled me inside the janitor's closet and told me to feed off him."

"And you did it? No problem?" Gillian proceeded cautiously. Although it was definitely none of her business, she felt she had to know. Addie would never bite an unwilling host. In fact, vampires seldom had unwilling participants, thanks to pheromones.

"Well, it took some persuasion on his part, but—"

"Did you enjoy it?" She couldn't help herself. And she knew she'd touched a nerve the moment that last word left her mouth. Addie's gaze shot up instantly.

"I was hungry." Her statement seemed simple, but Gillian could tell she was restraining herself.

"What about . . . you know . . . pleasure-wise?" Gillian knew she shouldn't keep pushing, but her curiosity was winning out.

"What do you mean?" Addie's eyes had darkened considerably.

"You hadn't fed directly from a host in how long?"

"Josh fed on me this morning, Gill. Forrest was the least of my problems."

"Oh. Okay." Gillian cleared her throat. Addie's mood today probably had a lot to do with the encounter with her ex. And she didn't want to touch *that* issue. "Well, after tonight, Dr. Wolfe won't have any of your trace in his system."

"Good. That's a relief."

"Is it?" Gillian asked before she could stop herself.

"What's that supposed to mean, Gillian?"

"I'm just saying that if you wanted to bite him again, maybe it would be better if your trace stayed in his system."

"I won't bite him again, Gillian. It was bad enough that it happened today. I could've hurt him. I shouldn't have let it happen."

"Then why did you?"

"I was hungry, weak, tired, and not thinking clearly. What other explanation do you need?" Addie stood up, pushing the chair back against the wall and making Gillian jump.

A vampire's temper was nothing to be trifled with. "I'm sorry, Addie. I didn't mean to upset you. I was just—I mean, we both know that you don't bite just anybody. There's a pleasure attached to it."

"I don't have feelings for Forrest, Gillian. I never have and I'm not about to start now. He's my friend, nothing more. What's your sudden interest?"

Well, Gillian had been wondering that herself.

"Nothing specific. I was just curious," she clarified, her eyes not quite meeting Addie's.

It was the truth, right?

Anyway, she wouldn't get time to think about it at the moment. She had begun shifting her weight in her chair. Her ankle had to be taken care of soon. "There was no time, Gillian. You haven't experienced the need to feed. An immortal would understand the difference."

"Oh, okay."

"I'm sorry. I didn't mean it like that."

"Yes, you did, Addie." Gillian lowered her head. She wondered just how long it would take for her friends to stop penalizing her for having an expiration date within her DNA.

"So, how are you feeling? You don't look so hot." Addie tried to sound sympathetic, but her need-to-know tone was something Gillian was all too familiar with. She was twenty years old, a college graduate, thanks to taking college courses while still in high school. This work had been the best distraction from dealing with her grief. But anyway, she had her own job, and the deed to the house had passed to her two years ago. When was Addie going to start treating her like an adult? Sure, she was immortal, but in human years, Addie still looked twenty-five. Gillian would catch her soon. It was high time Addie started treating her like an equal. "Oh, I'm good, just tired." Gillian made one last attempt to dodge the topic. There was no sense in worrying Addie over something that she wasn't sure warranted worrying about.

"You look like you had a rough night. And not for the first time, either. What's going on, Gillian? This isn't like you." Addie's look told her she wasn't getting out of this one. And this time, Dr. Wolfe wasn't there to provide a convenient distraction. She sighed.

"I've been having a lot of nightmares recently."

"About?"

"Sean."

"As in your ex, Sean?"

Gillian nodded.

"It's been four years, Gillian."

"So what? How long did it take you to get over your father turning you?"

"That was different. I didn't know who he was, let alone that he sent his immortal blood to Bridget instead of making an appearance himself. And Forrest even had to inject me with it! Not to mention that he just assumed I wanted to be immortal without asking. Immortal just like him."

Addie's cup landed forcefully on the kitchen table.

"Yeah, it sure sounds like you're over it, Addie."

"Your point?" Addie's eyes narrowed. "This has nothing to do with your dreams."

"My point is that it takes a long time to forgive and forget," Gillian finished, her mind on Sean. She wondered if she would even be able to sleep tonight.

"Sean made his own choice, Gillian."

"I wanted to be a vampire then, too."

"You were young, Gillian, you made a mistake. You can't really expect to find the love of your life at sixteen, can you? He knew better."

"How could he? I didn't know better. I just got a bad feeling is all."

"Well, he didn't bite you, did he?"

Gillian was sure that Addie noticed her hesitation to answer. She didn't want to share that tiny but important detail with her just yet. But she also didn't want to flat-out lie. So, she merely shrugged.

"That means you're not connected, and ergo, he doesn't know where you are. I'm right about that, aren't I?" Addie asked.

Gillian just shrugged once more. She wasn't sure if the connection was there to begin with. Otherwise she wouldn't have continued to live in Erie, hiding in plain sight. A simple spell had made her house invisible to his eyes, after a lot of practice. That should have been enough of a hint. He wouldn't be foolish enough to come back, would he? What would be the point? She had moved on. Hadn't he as well? But what else could explain the nightmares? Was Sean really visiting her in her dreams? What could he possibly want with her, after all this time? She didn't want to think about it anymore. "Are you all right taking the first shift with Forrest, Addie?"

She saw Addie's lips purse. She could tell she wanted more information. But how could Gillian give it to her when she didn't know the answers herself?

"We'll be all right. Get some sleep." Addie put a hand on her shoulder and squeezed. Gillian appreciated the reassurance of her touch.

"Okay. I'll see you at three, for a change." Gillian smiled at her, squeezing the vampire's other hand. She let out a soft laugh as she realized how cold Addie's skin felt. She guessed the long blood-abstinence was still affecting her. Her body would take a while to feel warm.

"Sounds good. And Gillian?"

"Yeah?"

"Thanks for your help today."

"Anytime." And Gillian meant it. She appreciated what Addie and Forrest had done for her. She always would.

Chapter 8

2009

"Ugh." Gillian tried to stretch, get ready for the morning. But everything hurt. She should've been used to it. It wasn't the first time she'd dealt with the consequences of a spell failure. She tried to sit up, but her head felt like it had been hit by a hammer, so she leaned against her pillow while she peeked out her window. Yep, the morning's brightness let her know it was definitely time to get up. And Addie would also be up.

She scoffed as she removed the purple covers, the color she had chosen, to honor her mother. She was a light blue kind of girl, the color representing a feeling of peacefulness she had the impression she would never achieve. But perhaps, this could be the gesture her mother would appreciate, and that would get her to talk to her daughter, finally, get some closure on why she simply couldn't stay.

Gillian sighed. Best to get the inevitable confrontation with Addie over with, like ripping off a Band-Aid. She gasped as she almost tripped over the sleeping lycan. *Of course—how else would I have made it to my bed from the attic?* She tried to fix her hair with her fingers until she figured it would probably be a lost cause. She reached for the purple robe sitting in the trunk at the foot of the bed.

"Hi, Gillian. Did you sleep well?" His sleepy gray eyes stared at her. She should've been nice and greeted him back. But she hadn't asked for his help. And he was invading her space! The fact that Addie had involved him, yet again, in her issues got on her nerves. She was embarrassed enough. There was no reason why the lycan should know about her failure as well.

"Oh, jeez!" she scoffed, her legs taking her around his sleeping form in the hallway and moving into the bathroom, slamming the door.

❖

"Ah, the teenager awakens." Addie looked up from her green coffee mug, although Gillian knew better than to assume it was holding the caffeinated drink. "Of course, if the teenager hadn't been in the attic, she would've been up at a more reasonable hour."

"The *teenager* almost got a heart attack this morning. Kindly tell Dr. Wolfe to get more suitable sleeping arrangements next time," Gillian stated, reaching into the cabinet for her cereal.

"You're going to need more than carbs after your little adventure yesterday. Eggs are on the stove. And I was on call yesterday; Forrest was just watching over you. I suggest you thank him, since he gave up his free night to come check on you." Gillian could tell Addie was working very hard to keep her voice restrained. *Too bad.*

"I'm fine, Addie. Nothing I haven't handled before." Gillian tried to shrug it off.

"Oh, you mean it worked this time?"

"It's a work in progress." Now Gillian was the one working on restraining her voice. Addie's mocking tone and blatant disregard for her magic abilities were making it very hard.

"It will be progress when you're able to get off the floor on your own. When Forrest doesn't have to carry you down."

"Well, I didn't ask him to do it! I would've been fine on my own." Gillian slammed her plate of eggs against the kitchen table, her fork and knife making a clattering sound against the crystal bowl. Was she imagining things, or were Addie's eyes turning misty?

"Yes, that's just fucking great." Addie stood up, towering over the blond witch. "You're lucky Forrest wanted to let you sleep, because I wanted to slap the unconsciousness right out of you! You promised to stop!"

"I need my mother! Why can't you understand that?" Her plea sounded like a baby's moan, but it would have to do when she was at her wit's end. And when Addie's vampire traits were becoming more pronounced.

"Bridget is dead, Gillian! No amount of magic will bring her back! You're giving up your energy, your lifeforce, for just a few minutes with her—and you're not even getting that! You could get seriously sick with burnout, even die . . . I'm sure Bridget warned you about the dangers of using too much magic."

That did it. Gillian couldn't contain her tears any longer. She didn't fight when Addie pulled her into her arms, her signature vanilla scent overpowering her senses.

"I'm sorry," she heard Addie whisper. "I know it's hard. But please." Gillian realized Addie had begun to tear up too when she felt warm drops start to accumulate on her forehead. "I can't lose you, too."

Chapter 9

2013

"**Y**ou couldn't tell her, could you?"

Gillian gasped and found herself unable to move, or even scream. Sean hovered above her.

"Well, of course not," he continued. "You can't tell her you're in this mess because you allowed me certain liberties once and then you decided everyone else was better off not knowing?"

"What—what do you want from me? Why now?" Gillian could feel the hairs at the back of her neck standing up. She was struggling to speak. It had been *four years*. How could he still do that to her? Couldn't he just leave her alone?

"I want what you promised. Eternal life."

"You have it!" she roared with all her might. She had to take a stab at making him feel like he made her feel: terrified, and even more terrified at what he was capable of doing.

"Ah, but someone is missing. I can't find you anywhere but your dreams. And even then, you're not pleased to see me."

Gillian continued to struggle, now breathing hard. Controlling her emotions was proving to be almost as much of a workout as trying to control her physical movements.

"Let go of me!" Her hands were pinned at either side of her pillow, her legs straight down in the middle of the bed. She felt like she was being restrained by an invisible apparatus. She could only move her hips like she was trying to exercise her abs. But right now, she didn't care how ridiculous she looked. She just wanted him out of her house. Out of her life.

"Can't. We have a bond, a bond that took me four years to perfect. Would've been easier with an immortal witch by my side, but no matter, I'll get my way soon enough. Plus, I've been told blood ages like the wine, gets better with age."

"What?" Gillian could feel sweat soaking through the back of her baby-blue tank top. Her breathing was still ragged, and now she was genuinely puzzled. Was there a connection? How had he harnessed it without her consent? Had Eric Callahan helped? Why now, after so long? Why was he so intent on feeding off her?

And could a witch still be a witch and become immortal by turning into a different species, such as a vampire or a werewolf? Her mother hadn't accepted—did she know something Gillian didn't?

"So many questions . . . too many to ponder alone. And I suppose I can't be of much help, considering how much you despise me, which is uncalled for considering how once you couldn't keep your hands

63

off me. I wonder, will Adelaide help? Or are you still too afraid of a vampire? You shouldn't be. After all, haven't your powers grown?"

"Screw you. Leave Addie out of this. I don't need her to take care of you," Gillian whispered, feeling a sudden surge of pride for finding her voice. He could have a connection, but she was a witch. And she would find a way to eliminate it, and him . . . permanently.

"Oh, confidence! I like that in my woman."

"I was never yours!"

"Wrong on both counts," Sean cackled. "The confidence isn't there, and our connection is. What would Addie and the lycan think of you now?"

"Leave them out of this!" Gillian gasped as she felt herself struggle to scream. This was her problem. She wouldn't involve her friends.

He whispered in her ear and she could feel the heat of his mouth. "I'm going to come back for you, Gillian, make no mistake." She tried to turn her head, but he still found a way to make bile rise into her mouth. "You belong to me."

❖

"Gillian! Gillian, wake up!"

Gillian opened her eyes, feeling dizzy. The sun was just beginning to brighten the sky outside as light came through the high basement windows. The room spun, and she slumped off her chair onto the floor.

Her eyes began to clear, and she saw Forrest squatting next to her, looking worried. "How did you . . ." Gillian looked at Forrest's cage. Where was its door? She groaned as she discovered the bent metal by the bottom of the wooden basement stairs. It had taken the three of them a long time to put that together. Magic didn't help with hands-on work, and her father had assembled all the furniture that required it once upon a time. Thankfully, despite keeping a home free from most of her mother's memories, she hadn't gotten rid of her father's tools. Maybe she'd been hoping against hope that he'd come back from wherever he was now and would want them back.

"Sorry, but you were gasping and struggling, and I heard you scream. Are you all right?"

"Fine, um, thanks." She smiled thinly and attempted to fold her legs back under her in a more dignified manner.

"Let me help."

"I'm fine, Dr. Wolfe, you're the one who should be resting." Gillian's attempt to stand up failed. Forrest grabbed her and set her back on the chair. She bit her lip as she felt pain pulsate from her ankle. Contrary to her hopes, it seemed that it was just as swollen as the night before.

"Your ankle?"

"It's fine, just—"

"Swollen. And painful." He crouched down in front of her. "I'm assuming you already took something for it?"

"Advil. I'm sure the swelling will go away on its own." Gillian shifted uncomfortably on the chair.

"Not if you keep walking on it. I'll go get some ice."

"No need." Gillian put her hand on Forrest's arm before he could get on his feet. "I got it." She conjured the bag of ice with a simple wrist circled movement.

Yes, complicated spells required incantations, like summoning her mother from another world. But once she practiced magic enough, she could make a simple movement to get what she wanted. Of course, her lifeforce did still get affected. But it was such a small thing that she barely felt her heartbeat increase, as her body looked for an alternate source of energy to free the magic without weakening her. She would have to go to sleep today anyway, and her energy would return. Still, using too much magic energy would interfere with her healing, so she'd better take it easy with magic today.

"Now you're just showing off," Forrest chuckled.

"It didn't help much on the stairs yesterday. Sorry about that."

"I wasn't the one who got hurt." Forrest put her right foot onto his knee and pressed the ice into her swollen ankle. "Swelling should go down provided you keep it elevated and on ice, and limit movement. No stairs at work. Do you have an ankle brace? Unless, can you heal yourself, you know, magically?"

"No," Gillian laughed. "Older witches used to, until one of them tried to cheat death. She was sick, and would heal herself every time she felt weak. It brought her reprieve, for a while. But death, it's a destiny. For most of us anyway. Of course, I'm not even close to that kind of power. I'm just a beginner by witchcraft standards. But the point is that life, the decisions that come with granting it and taking it, that was never what the powers were intended for, so I guess the universe found a way to even the score. I can't even help heal you. Imagine that, no need for doctors." Forrest's hand pressed the ice further into her ankle and she inhaled sharply. As far as she was concerned, the painkiller could kick in any time now.

"Sorry. It'll help," he assured her. "But yeah, I'd be out of a job, so we wouldn't want that."

"There's a way to restore life—I guess that's what we'd call it."

"Sorry?" Forrest glanced at her. She swore she could see the wheels of his scientist-brain turning.

"A witch can trade her life, so another can live," she said softly. Her brows furrowed as Forrest set down the bag of ice, his gray eyes now fixed on hers.

"You can do that?"

"It takes a tremendous amount of focus and it drains the life from you, but I like to think I'd be capable of it if I had a worthy cause." She flinched as the ice came in contact with her ankle again. She tried to focus on the drops of water that had fallen to the stone floor.

"What about the people you'd leave behind?"

"My mother never cared about that, so why would I?" Gillian shook her head as she realized the tone of voice she had used. Forrest didn't deserve the pent-up anger inside her. That was solely reserved for Sean . . . and her mother. "Sorry."

"It's all right." Forrest cleared his throat. "But just so you know, your mother cared about you very much. And she's not the only one."

"Yeah, sure." Gillian feigned disinterest. But she would be lying if she said she had no interest in what he was going to say, as his gray eyes settled on hers, his hand grasping her own.

"Good morning." Addie appeared at the bottom of the stairs in her red robe and furry black cat slippers. "I'm sorry, did I interrupt?"

"Not at all," Forrest responded before Gillian could. "Just dealing with ankle issues."

"Ah, so that's what happened last night that you didn't want to tell me about." To anyone else, Addie's tone might have sounded casual, but Gillian knew beneath it there was a hint of anger. Addie hated when she was kept uninformed.

"I didn't want to bother you."

"Come on, Gillian, I could see a mile away you were trying not to limp. Endearing, but hardly effective. What happened?" Addie crossed her arms, leaning against the metal rail of the basement staircase.

"She tripped on her cat's tail, an accident. She'll be fine," Forrest responded.

Gillian bit her lip. This was just what Forrest always did. When he sensed a hint of temper between them, he'd intervene. She didn't know if she found it thoughtful or annoying. Right now, she was leaning towards the latter. Just because she wasn't immortal didn't mean she couldn't deal with her own issues.

"See that she is. Speaking of which, how are you feeling, Forrest?"

Gillian detected a slight change of tone in Addie's voice, a more intimate one. "I'm fine, Addie. Great, actually, thanks to Gillian." He smiled at her. For the life of her, Gillian could never get a read on him. She had been sixteen the last time she couldn't get a read on a man. And that situation hadn't ended so well. Perhaps that was why she shied away from analyzing her feelings for the handsome lycan as much as possible.

"Good. Catch." Addie threw Forrest a bag of blood.

"Why are you giving me your food?" He furrowed his eyebrows.

"You don't want it?" Addie sounded pleasantly surprised.

"Why would I?"

"If you had any vampire trace left, you would," Gillian clarified, smiling as she realized what Addie was up to.

"Welcome back, Wolfe." Addie punched him playfully on the shoulder. "I'll take that back."

"Well, now that everything is back to normal, I'll be at work." Work suddenly sounded very appealing. Gillian stood up from her chair before either of her friends could offer assistance. If they were back to their playful behavior, she really shouldn't be there.

"Gillian, let me help—"

But Gillian had zoomed to her room before Forrest could finish his sentence.

Chapter 10

2009

G illian could taste the faint flavor of chocolate chip ice cream when he kissed her. She was more of a sherbet type of gal, orange usually being the flavor of the day. But as long as they were kissing, she didn't mind. He had a way of holding her that took her breath away.

She breathed in as their lips parted for air, and she couldn't resist leaning against his ever-present brown jacket. He put his arm around her, pulling her further against him while kissing her forehead.

"I swear your hair color changes on a daily basis, Gillian," he whispered, smiling.

"It gets darker the more powers I master. You know that, Sean." Gillian focused on the thread of hair draped across her shoulder. The cool sunset cast its dirty blond color with a golden hue. It was one of those perfect days in Erie, cool and breezy, but not cold. These were rare in the fall, so she had taken advantage and hung out outside after school with the boy she loved.

"Actually, I didn't. There are a lot of things I don't know about you. When are you going to let me in?"

"What's that supposed to mean?" Didn't they share everything?

"See, this is what I don't get about you. You come up with sudden plans, think everything will figure itself out, and then you change your mind. You don't want today what you wanted yesterday. It's hard to keep up with you."

"Sean, what are you talking about?"

"Here's the thing: immortality is great, but I accepted it only on the condition you'd be with me. So I get turned—a painful process with a really ugly man behind the pheromones, might I add, biting me—while you were at the hospital with a dying Bridget instead of being with me for moral support. We spend a steamy night together, and the next day you're nowhere to be found. What am I supposed to think?"

"Sean, my mom . . ." Gillian couldn't help the tears now blurring her vision.

"She dies and you suddenly change your mind? You can hide it all you want, but it won't erase the night we spent together. I own you."

Gillian stiffened.

"I'm coming back for you," he whispered. "You just wait."

❖

Gillian gasped as the sound of the office door opening

jarred her awake. To her horror, she saw a pencil float up from her desk and speed towards her visitor, moving at a faster pace than she could control right now. Her focus was currently nowhere to be found. It was a surgeon, judging by his scrub cap, and he moved his head slightly to avoid it. She would've sighed in relief if she hadn't set sight on the surgeon's misty blue eyes.

"Josh, don't you knock?" It wasn't as if they were friends.

"Jeez, Gillian, I know you don't like me very much, but throwing potentially lethal things at me is a little drastic, don't you think?"

"I'm a witch, Josh. A pencil through the heart would be awfully messy on a white tile floor, wouldn't you agree?"

"And here I thought your office had an open-door policy." He didn't seem offended in the slightest.

"For the one who broke Addie's heart? Try again." Gillian crossed her arms and stood up. Josh gave her an uneasy feeling whenever he was around.

"I'm not the one who ended it. That was her doing."

"And I suppose you had nothing whatsoever to do with that?" Gillian hated when he did this, trying to sound ever so blameless. Someone else might buy it, but she was too well acquainted with Josh's habits.

"Well, I'm not the one biting lycans, am I?" His smirk told her he couldn't wait to bring that one up. No wonder Addie had looked more than mildly upset last night.

"To tell the truth, Josh, I'd rather not get into those details."

"Tell me the werewolf has a thing for you and not Addie."

Now *that* she wasn't expecting.

She let out the deep breath she didn't know she was holding. Why was he asking? Had Forrest told him something?

"Why would I tell you that?" She tried to sound as calm and nonchalant as possible.

"Because I asked politely, and I want to know."

She sighed as she took her seat. "Well, I'm sorry to disappoint."

"Look, next to Addie, you're the one he spends the most time with and maybe you haven't noticed, but he does look pretty darn nervous around you."

"Maybe he trusts Addie more that he trusts me. Did that ever occur to you?"

"With that look he gives you, it's not a trust issue, I can tell you that."

"I thought you immortals never looked beyond your own species. Good gracious, are you telling me I've been wrong all these years?" Gillian was seldom sarcastic, but she knew the best way to end a conversation with Josh was by annoying him.

"Maybe we don't, but whoever made lycans immortal did not make a meaningful contribution if you ask me. Oh, did I strike a nerve?"

Gillian cleared her throat. Josh's last remark about immortality had brought her nightmare back to her mind. But that was not a topic she was going to discuss with Addie's ex.

"Well, seems like you have your mind made up. Why bother to consult with me then?"

"You haven't confirmed it. Why don't we make it snappy? I've got surgery soon and I'd like to spend it figuring out how to get Addie back. That stupid lycan. She always did have a soft spot for him, and they were friends when I first asked her out, I know. I get it, he saved her life and all, but enough already, I mean—"

"Gillian, do you have a minute?" Gillian looked beyond Josh to find Forrest by her door. He was carrying a bunch of roses wrapped in brown paper.

"Dr. Wolfe, of course. What can I do for you?" Gillian smiled at him.

Josh turned to face him. "Oh yes, Dr. Lycan Wolfe, what can we do for you? Do come in! It's not as if you're interrupting anything."

"Hello, Josh. I apologize, am I interrupting your feeding?" Forrest sounded forcefully polite. After Josh's earlier low blow, Gillian couldn't blame him. She wouldn't even mind if he punched the cocky vampire. But she had a feeling that with Forrest's excessive politeness, forcefully polite was as good as it was going to get. Better for her, she supposed. She wasn't in the mood for an immortal fistfight in her office.

"Oh, no, Addie took care of me yesterday. But I appreciate your concern." Josh's tone was laced with disdain. Gillian had half a mind to get out and let them sort out their issues, but leaving them alone could result in another mess she didn't have the time, or frankly, the will, to clean up today.

"Yeah, anytime." Forrest tried to brush past him.

"And as I understand it, after she took care of me, you took care of her." Josh was again in front of the werewolf.

"Josh, don't." Gillian tried, as diplomatically as she could muster, to break into what was surely going to be an ugly argument.

"Don't get me wrong, I'm touched," he continued. "She must have been desperate to drink your—see, I don't know, should I call it blood? Since it's badly compromised, I'd rather not."

"Whatever you choose to call it, it saved her," said Forrest. "If you care about her like you say you do, you should've known better than to feed off her when she was between two surgeries. You endangered Addie and her patient, although I doubt that crossed your mind once you got your fix."

Forrest took Gillian by the arm and pulled her back behind him. She hoped it wasn't because he planned to punch the vampire.

"I tried to avoid it. I called the witch," Josh said defensively.

"No, you called her office. She had the day off and no one else knows how to clean up your mess."

"I bet she knew just how to clean yours."

Gillian saw the look in Josh's eyes. He was way too calm. Something was wrong.

"So help me, I swear—"

Gillian grabbed Forrest's arm as he took a step toward Josh. She had rarely seen him this angry before. She had better put a stop to it before something other than veiled anger surfaced. "Dr. Wolfe, it's not worth it."

She heard Forrest sigh, but he stopped moving. Josh looked genuinely surprised. "Wow, I stand corrected."

"Excuse me?" Gillian swore she heard Forrest growl.

"Oh, come on! You don't want Addie. You want the little witch that comes with the package. Got to admit, I'm not surprised; your standards were always questionable. Not sure if she sees you that way, though. Oh, wow!" Josh feigned surprise. "She's right behind you. Why don't I ask her if she likes dogs?"

"Yes, please do." Gillian kept her hand on the werewolf's arm.

"Pardon me?" Josh's frown told her he wasn't expecting her to actually take part in the conversation.

"Well, we both know werewolves look more like creatures from Greek myths, not dogs. And as you pointed out, Dr. Wolfe is the exception, thanks to me of course. Magic can work wonders with lycan abilities and looks. So he looks cuter, not as intimidating. Can't say it would work with you though." Gillian grinned devilishly.

Gillian would later apologize profusely to the werewolf. Forrest sucked a deep breath, his body frame stiffening slightly as her arms made their way up his back. She could feel his body heat through his scrub top.

"Oh, you did that?" Josh squinted at her and shrugged. "Now I'm slightly disappointed. Here I thought it was just simple evolution. Oh well, should've known better. Evolution doesn't mess with lycans."

"Yes, well, magic does have its pros as well, Dr. Ambrose," Gillian pointed out, moving to stand next to the werewolf. She felt his arm settle softly around her waist.

Good boy.

"Josh Ambrose, what will it take to get you into surgery?"

Gillian distanced herself from Forrest the minute she heard Addie's voice. When had she come in?

Why hadn't she heard her? *This lack of sleep is going to kill me.*

"Addie! To what do I owe the pleasure?" Josh's attention immediately shifted.

"You heard me. Surgery in thirty."

"You could've just had one of the nurses come get me," Josh said, winking at her.

Gillian sighed. It seemed that Josh was in the mood to get on everyone's nerves today.

"Because that always works so well. And what are you doing here? If I remember correctly, I fed you yesterday," Addie pointed out with barely concealed resentment.

"How could I forget? No, nothing like that. Let's just say I had a question that only Gillian could answer."

"Fine. Are we done here?"

Josh glanced at Gillian.

"Yep, we pretty much are," he answered.

"Grand. I'll see you down there, Forrest. Ooh, red roses, nice touch." Addie glanced at the flowers in Forrest's grip.

"Yeah, in a minute." Forrest smiled at her, looking a little befuddled.

"Great. And I'll see you at lunch, Gill."

Gillian just nodded. She couldn't help but heave a sigh of relief as the two vampires left her office.

"Dr. Wolfe, I'm sorry."

"And I'll see you at lunch as well. These are for you, Addie told me how much you like them, and thank you for your help last night." Forrest hurriedly put the flowers on her desk.

"How are you feeling?" Gillian smiled as she caught their scent.

"Never better." He smiled back.

"Just doing my job." Gillian shifted uncomfortably. Part of the reason she hadn't gone into nursing was that she preferred to work behind the scenes. There was no better place for a low profile than the lab. That way, she could follow in her mother's footsteps as a witch and as a health worker, but hopefully not suffer her fate.

"Yeah, I know. What Addie wants, she gets." Forrest looked chaffed.

"No, that's not what I meant," Gillian said exasperatedly.

"No worries. I'll see you later."

"Dr. Wolfe, about earlier . . ." She caught him just as he was making his way out the door.

"Yeah, Josh has some nerve, doesn't he?" Forrest smiled at her. "Hopefully, he'll piss off for a while."

"Yeah, but—"

"No worries. I get it. I'll see you later, Gillian."

Gillian smiled and waved at him as he left. As she turned around and caught sight of the forgotten pencil on the floor, a feeling of dread settled at the pit of her stomach.

Did Sean really know where she was? Would he come back?

Chapter 11

"You told her I told you how much she liked roses? Way to go, Captain Smooth," said Addie as she lay back on her seat.

"Well, what was I supposed to say? It's true!"

Addie sighed. Poor Forrest. He really had no clue when it came to women.

"Forrest, you know how it goes. If you have nothing to say that will put the odds in your favor, don't say anything at all," she said, as if it was the most obvious thing in the world. Maybe for her, but Forrest still looked lost. "Look, having told her that, you made it sound like it was my idea when, in fact, it wasn't."

"Technically you had something to do with it."

"She doesn't need to know I helped you, Forrest! I just put some details into place." Addie tried to relax into her chair. She was really trying not to sound exactly like she was feeling, which was, frankly, annoyed. Fingers crossed Forrest wouldn't notice. But when it came to women, despite his handsome frame and boyish looks, Forrest needed some serious help.

"This is useless." Forrest buried his face in his hands.

"Forrest—"

"She'll never go for it."

"You don't know that, Forrest!"

But Gillian was another matter. For one thing, she didn't have immortality. Second, the odds of Forrest actually going out with Gillian, especially since, according to the witch, she was still afraid of her ex— Addie really didn't want to squash his hopes. But they looked pretty slim.

"She toned down your lycan rage."

"Because you asked her to," Forrest pointed out.

"You wouldn't ask her!"

"Oh yeah, that would've gone over really well. *Hi, Gillian, this is a little awkward since we're only friends by association, but I realize that when I'm on my true werewolf form, I could really hurt you. So, since you're a witch and all, I figure maybe you could do something about that. I would really appreciate it. And by the way, when this is over, do you think we could go out to dinner and get to know each other better? Because you know, I really like you.*"

"There you go! What's wrong with that?" Sure, a little rough around the edges, Addie thought, but she knew Gillian appreciated genuine.

"It wouldn't work!" Forrest was normally so optimistic. "If I thought I had a shot I would've tried it."

"Tried *what?* All you can do in her presence is smile and nod!"

"That is not true. We talk."

"Right." Although she had to admit there had been slight improvement in Forrest and Gillian's relationship, she would not concede the argument. "But you barely know her. Gillian's been secretive and sort of introverted since her mother died. I can't blame her. But give yourself a chance. She might surprise you."

"I bet."

"What's that?" Addie leaned forward on her chair.

"You know Josh wants to get back together with you, right?"

"Oh, he can go screw him—"

"Hi." It was Gillian.

Addie pursed her lips. She was careful not to swear over her young adoptee if she could help it. "Hey, Gill. You okay?"

"Yeah. I was typing and screening blood. Sorry I missed lunch."

"No problem," said Addie. "We know better than to venture into your office at lunchtime anyway. You hungry? I'm sure we can go get you something now."

"No, thanks. Got administrative stuff to take care of. I'll make it up to you, though. Dinner tonight?"

"Can't. On call tonight."

"Oh, okay. Are you working too, Dr. Wolfe?"

"Pardon?"

Addie had to resist the urge to laugh as she saw Forrest's eyes open wide. He clearly was not expecting the invitation. She feared that he was taking the "friend by association" label way too seriously. Then again, although Forrest and Gillian had eaten lunches by themselves when her surgeries had run over, Gillian had never actually invited him to dinner.

"Do you also have to work tonight?"

"Nope. He's free after his next surgery, as it turns out," Addie answered when it was clear that Forrest was still in shock. She didn't want Gillian to think he was being cold or dismissive.

"Oh, good, I was hoping to talk to you anyway. Got any favorite places?" Gillian leaned against the door.

"What?"

"Dinner? I'm sorry. I assumed you wanted to go."

Addie cleared her throat while she kicked Forrest discreetly on the ankle.

"Oh, of course!" That seemingly snapped him out of his reverie as he flinched and, with a low grunt, moved away from Addie's side. "Sorry, got that surgery on my mind. Anything you like is fine by me, Gillian."

"I usually go with Chinese."

"That's fine." Forrest smiled.

"What time do you get out of surgery?"

"Around 8:00 p.m., if everything goes well."

"All right. Just swing by my office when you're done."

"I'll be there." His smile widened.

"Great. It's too bad you can't come, Addie." Gillian glanced at her.

"Another time. You kids enjoy." Addie couldn't resist giving her a big smile, even if her vampire incisors stood out. There was no one in the hallway at the moment anyway.

"I'll hold you to it," Gillian promised as her glance went back to Forrest. "I'll see you later tonight, Dr. Wolfe."

"Yeah, I look forward to it," Forrest said, still smiling.

"Oh, and thanks for the roses. They're beautiful." Gillian peeked back through the door before trotting down the hallway at her usual fast pace.

Addie's chair turned to face Forrest. "I'm looking forward to it too," she chuckled as the werewolf blushed.

"Let it go, Addie. It's not like it's a date. She invited you first. Fat chance of that happening anyway."

"That doesn't mean it can't turn into one."

"Right."

"Oh, come on, Wolfie! You can't honestly tell me you don't know how to do this! Sure, it's been a long time since you took someone out on a date instead of the usual hospital Christmas party. Seriously, though, when was the last time you spent time with someone you were really interested in?" Addie started to wiggle her pen as she leaned back into her desk chair. This was bound to be interesting.

"Well, there was that ICU nurse."

"Mindy?"

"Her name was Melinda and I never called her that."

"Come on, Forrest! Seriously?"

"Yeah. What? You didn't like her?"

"She was fine." Addie shrugged, clearing her throat as she realized she was deviating from the subject. "That's not the point and you know it."

"You're right. Well, I took *you* to my parents' house after I dated Melinda, so that sort of counts." Forrest looked pensive for a moment.

"That does not count. We weren't dating."

"Not for lack of them trying. According to my parents, you're the perfect vampire specimen."

"Yeah, not gonna happen. They just know I owe you a debt, so in vampire versus lycan terms, I cannot harm you or them," Addie pointed out.

After all, friendship aside, the enmity between vampires and lycans was legendary. Forrest's parents would've been fools not to consider those consequences when Forrest told them about Bridget's plan. Or, to be more specific, Gregory Brystol's plan for his estranged daughter—his choice that Bridget Cassidy had orchestrated by talking to Addie's mother about her impending deployment.Except. . .would he have told them? After all, he was making her his mortal enemy. Except that he also had saved her life, which was the spark that began their friendship. In the hospital, they had gotten along as colleagues, but a debt like the one she owed him. . .That transcended immortality itself, would bind them together forever. And he had risked his career and medical license if anyone had found out. Yes, immortality existed, but it wasn't advertised. It was treated like a religion of sorts; some believed, some didn't. If the proverbial secret got out, a lot of powerful people would pay large incentives to have immortality in their arsenal. And as Bridget had pointed out once upon a time, balance kept life going. An unbalance favoring immortality would be disastrous for both living and undead species. Without mortals, vampires could not feed and would cease to exist due to starvation. Yes, immortals could feed off each other when in a pickle, but that did not sustain them long-term, as lycan blood was compromised by the lycanthrope virus and vampires' blood was not really their own. Loss of blood acted like the balancing act; some mortals weakened, some died, and some became immortal. But all numbers had a limit. And immortality was not an exception. "Addie, do you really think I'm keeping tabs on that? I don't care—"

And she knew he didn't. But would his parents? Stephen and Margaret Wolfe had not given her that inkling so far. But them not advertising they were aware of Addie's debt to their son didn't mean they wouldn't hold that over her head if ever a time came.

But that didn't mean they needed to worry about it now.

"Anyway, who ended it between you and Melinda?"

"It just wasn't working out is all."

"You mean you did."

"I was the one who brought it up. Where are you going with this, Addie?"

"That you haven't seriously dated in a while. Don't you want to get back into it?"

"Not with Gillian. I don't want to ruin our friendship. Besides, she's known me since she was a kid, wouldn't that be . . . kind of creepy for her? Not to mention the issue of mortality. She's uninterested in immortality. What kind of future would that be?"

"The kind that you won't find out about if you don't try."

"Whatever, Addie, it's just dinner." He raised his hands and stood up.

"All right," she sighed. "To surgery you go."

Addie watched him leave the room. She wasn't fooled. She had seen how he acted around Gillian. But he did have a point. If those two ever got together, the complications could be bigger than the rewards. And what did Gillian think? She had never said anything about Forrest. Not to mention her last relationship with an immortal had ended rather badly.

Addie scoffed. That was the understatement of the century. It had ended so badly he was still haunting her. But why? And more importantly, how?

Chapter 12

2007

"Incoming!"

Young doctor Forrest Wolfe barely had time to put gloves on before the straps started flooding the med tent.

"What have we got?" he asked, hoping one of the incoming strap carriers would have a minute to answer him.

Wait. Hadn't a convoy of nurses gone out this morning to a nearby post to help out with their medical shortage until the next med unit arrived that afternoon?

Had Addie been in that convoy?

"The convoy . . . a road grenade. Hit with shrapnel . . . casualties—more coming. Get in here quickly! Help them!" A hard-breathing African American corporal, judging by the bars pinned on his military uniform, had barely finished informing him when he ran out of the tent, presumably to get more bodies out of the battered Humvee.

"Don't know how many are gonna make it—they're in pretty bad shape—"

"Which convoy was it?" Forrest grabbed the young female private that was bringing the next strap by her shoulders.

"I don't know—only saw the fire! Move!" The young private maneuvered to get under Forrest's arms and ran out of the tent.

"Shit." Forrest wiped his forehead with the back of his forearm. The way these bodies looked—they needed morphine. There is no way they would survive an emergency surgery to repair whatever artery had been shattered, not to mention limbs.

Could any of them be saved? And where was Addie? Where was the convoy?

Was she back yet?

"Doctor! We got a pulse here! But she might need her legs amputated!" One of the nurses called him as she pressed gauzes on what Forrest could identify as an abdominal region covered in red. More amputations.

Would this war never end?

How much blood had this person lost? How much would they have left? "Doctor!"

He sighed as he reached for the saw.

"Don't stay here! They are dying!"

Forrest gasped as he set his eyes on the pale, green-eyed nurse on the gurney, whose breathing was loud despite the blood loss.

"My God, Addie!"

"Doctor, we have to stop the bleeding!" the green-clad nurse screamed at him.

"No!" He suddenly began breathing heavily, feeling his heart thumping in his ears, the screaming soldiers seemingly a thousand miles away. Even if he could save Addie's life at this point, she would never be whole again. And an amputation would produce more blood loss. Even if he removed her damaged legs, how much shrapnel would remain? How likely was she to live? Would she want to live this way? Bridget surely didn't think so.

"The insurance policy," he whispered.

There would be no more opportunities. The time was now.

"Doctor!"

"We got to move her," he whispered.

"No time! We're losing her! We've got to act now!" the nurse pleaded.

But there was no way he could do it here. Not with everyone watching.

"No. I can save her legs, but I've got to move her. I—cannot work like this," Forrest answered. Lame, especially in the military, but a lame excuse would do over a possible court martial for refusing to follow medical procedure. "I'll take her. I've got to take her to a more sterile environment. Move!" Forrest pushed the nurse away, taking Addie in his arms, his own clothing now turning crimson. He had to get to his tent. That was where the vial was. And he had to move quickly.

❖

He could hear Addie's weak moans as he put her on top of his sleeping bag. As a doctor, he had insisted on his own quarters so he would not disturb others with his equipment and medical calls. As he was the one that offered to move away from the barracks, the others had not made a fuss about it, thank goodness. In fact, they had probably thought him gay. But the Don't Ask, Don't Tell policy protected those people, so he could hide under that umbrella for now. He could feel Addie trembling as he tore up her military-issued top along with the brown top she wore underneath, now so soaked with blood he could probably wring it.

How was she still breathing?

It would not be for long, as the shallow nature of the breaths had slowed, and her eyes were glassy, looking at him, but not really.

"Hold on Addie. I'll get you through this," he whispered, as her body trembles became sporadic.

He reached for his medical bag, the only piece of equipment along with a standard issue gun that would be expected, never questioned, and never looked at. He sighed as he looked at the vial, using the little light he had. The tent was dark, on purpose. Being weakened by sunlight was not an option for a medic in a war zone. And a young, newborn vampire ran the risk of getting too weak, enough to not survive the transformation.

Before long, Gregory Brystol's blood was in a syringe, for his daughter. Normally the vampire would bite the host himself, but Gregory had walked away when Addie was born. Nobody knew where he was, and how had he found out that his daughter enlisted and got in contact with Addie's mother was a mystery, although everyone suspected the former couple still talked, despite Dorothy

Brystol denying it every time. And Gregory knew Bridget, Dorothy's best friend from nursing school, knew about their complicated relationship and continued contact.

"Bridget, I hope this works," he whispered.

Addie gave a small moan of pain as Forrest pressed against her chest and a trace of blood squirted out. She was pale, but he had to truly make sure she was literally on the brink of death. Otherwise, her father's blood itself would kill her, and the transformation would never take place. If he was risking a court martial for saving a young army nurse the unconventional way, through making sure she survived by cutting off her mortal circulation and replacing it with something undead, she better make it out, *appearing* alive at least. So he tore her military-issued trousers as well. And as for her legs . . . the pants were the only thing holding them in. He better take care of that before gangrene set in. But there was no way it would if her heart had stopped bea—

"Addie?"

When had the shallow breaths stopped?

He sighed as he looked at her. Her pale face was covered with sweat. One more press of the chest. . . No response to the pain it would surely have caused. Now was the time. Before he lost her for good. If he had not done so already.

"Hold on, my friend."

He slammed the needle into the heart. If there was no circulation, the blood would revive it, but it had to be at its source. It was his only shot.

"Come on."

His fist was ready to hit the heart, make sure the circulation started. But Bridget had warned him. Too much blood too quickly would kill her.

He had done his part.

The rest was up to her, and even if it took her the whole day, he wouldn't give up on her.

"You're so young. If anyone has a chance, it's you."

Of course, that was easy to say for someone born just on the brink of World War I, the war to end all wars, as his father would say.

How many wars had there been after? Weren't they in one now?

Had Gregory Brystol fought?

Would he have known his daughter would?

Would she die for this? Her first deployment?

"Come on, Addie," Forrest pleaded, his eyes closing in exhaustion, defeat.

She wasn't moving.

How long could he wait before someone grew suspicious? That military nurse had certainly opened her mouth by now, his weird, one could say erratic behavior, certainly noticed.

CRACK!

The sudden noise made Forrest jump out of his seated position.

His eyes opened wide as more, faster cracks, disturbed his quiet focus.

Her bones . . . readjusting.

"Welcome back, Addie," he whispered, smiling, as he took his friend's now cold hand. He was rewarded with a strong squeeze in return.

And so reality sunk in.

Yes, he had kept her alive. But what kind of life was

this? Would she want it? In his haste to prove he was as good as his word, he never had wondered. Would Adelaide Brystol want this kind of life?

"Forgive me, my friend," he said, pressing her hand to his cheek, where a tear now stained the perfect pale skin of her knuckles.

Chapter 13

2013

"Oh boy," Gillian sighed as she splashed water on her face. One look at the mirror in the women's restroom and she knew there was no way she would be able to cover the bags under her eyes tonight. Unless she used her magic for aesthetic purposes.

Ugh. The idea of using magic right now threatened to give her a migraine.

She sighed once again as she changed from her scrubs to jeans and a violet tee. Her mother had always said it was polite to change out of dirty work clothes before heading home. This time, the advice was awfully convenient. She wouldn't have liked to go to dinner wearing scrubs.

One more look at the mirror had her groaning in frustration. Sure, she could do her best to comb her hair and apply a pound of makeup, but the truth was that her immortal friend wouldn't have to bother because no matter how many hours Forrest spent in surgery, he would come out looking as handsome as ever.

Gillian turned her head as she caught herself form that line of thought. She'd accepted the fact that she would always feel underdressed in Addie's presence, but since when did she look at Forrest that way? Sure, he had never been ugly, but to actually admit . . .

She let out a small chuckle. The events of the morning combined with her lack of sleep and that hair-creeping feeling at the back of her neck whenever she so much as contemplated Sean were not exactly doing wonders for her relaxation. She really needed a night free of nightmares. She might have to concoct a potion for that one. An incantation probably would not work . . . well, maybe if she wanted to fall asleep in the attic.

Ah, another stab from the migraine. Glancing at her watch, she saw she had at least forty-five minutes before Forrest was finished with his shift. That was, provided everything was going well in surgery, and she assumed it was, since she hadn't heard a code blue. She figured almost an hour was more than enough time to catch a quick nap and, with any luck, she would both look and feel better before going to dinner.

Taking her blue-patched quilt out of her locker, Gillian lay down on the couch as soon as she reached her office. She sighed as her eyes drifted closed. Yes, a nap would be just what the doctor ordered.

❖

"Forrest, what is it?" Addie asked into the phone and yawned as she stretched out in the on-call room.

"Sorry, I didn't mean to wake you."

"It's fine. What?"

"Gillian is, um ..."

"Yeah?" Addie tried to prompt him without sounding too bothered. She hated being woken up in the middle of REM sleep. It was bad enough she wasn't sleeping in her coffin. And, and now she wasn't going to get even a semi-rest. *This better be important.*

"She's asleep and I don't want to wake her." Forrest sounded horribly distressed for a situation that didn't warrant it, in Addie's opinion. *Well, you woke me up.*

This wasn't a surprise. Based on what Gillian had told her yesterday, she had to be quite sleep-deprived. She knew Gillian wouldn't have confided in her unless she thought she had done everything in her power to try to fix it herself. Ever since her mother had died, Gillian had been almost compulsively independent. You couldn't blame her. If she was having a good sleep, Addie knew better than to disturb her, even if that meant cancelling dinner.

"Um, okay. Did you bring the Volvo?" Addie got out of bed, passing her hand through her hair. Even as a vampire, bed hair was an issue she couldn't escape.

"Yeah." Sometimes Forrest got the ridiculous idea to jog home after work. If he asked very nicely, she would even jog with him, provided the weather was cooperative. Living in Pennsylvania as a vampire had some advantages; pure sunny blue days were hard to come by. But living by the Great Lakes meant lots of winter weather, and being immortal didn't make her immune to twisted ankles from ice on the sidewalks. She would heal, but that didn't make the event any less painful. But Forrest was quick and agile, and an immortal birth had its advantages in that Forrest usually had more energy than her, especially when it had been more than eight hours without feeding. Today, however, she was grateful that he had his car on the premises.

"All right. Is she in deep?"

"She isn't stirring."

"Good. Get your keys and jacket. I'll scoop her up and you can drive her home. We shouldn't wake her. I'll order Chinese and have it delivered."

"Okay."

❖

Forrest glanced at Gillian. His brows furrowed as he detected a hint of movement. As quietly as he could muster, he walked over to her side. He couldn't help but notice the perspiration on her forehead. He got on his knees to check her temperature. She was twitching a little.

Gillian moaned.

A nightmare? Maybe I should wake her up. He glanced at the door. *Where's Addie?*

"Gillian?" He sighed in frustration. All the medical education in the world hadn't taught him how to handle this situation.

"No!" Gillian screamed, and the werewolf startled backward. She sprung forward from the couch and slipped. He caught her by her waist. *Thank goodness for lycan reflexes.*

"Gillian? Are you okay?" She was shaking and her back felt damp from sweat. She was also crying.

"Dr. Wolfe?" she whispered against her sobs.

"I'm here." He hoped he sounded soothing.

"I'm sorry."

Forrest had to strain to hear that one between the sobs. "No worries. I'll stay here if you want. I can drive you home when you're ready." He held his hand against her back, hoping again it would have a soothing effect.

"I'm sorry I got you into this. I won't let him hurt you."

"Hey, hey, Gillian, I'm safe. What are you talking about?" His palms were damp now too. He looked down at her face. She looked so vulnerable. "I'm immortal. I don't get hurt easily."

"But the silver. . .it will kill you." Gillian still sounded agitated.

"It's okay, Gillian. I'm okay." He put his hand on hers. "You had a nightmare."

She reached up to touch his face. "Damn it, he's right," Gillian whispered.

"About what? Gillian, what happened in your dream?"

"I don't particularly want to talk about it, Dr. Wolfe," she said, her hands dropping to her sides, "but I appreciate your concern."

"Okay. I hope you know I'm always here for you," he said quietly.

"You can't protect me. No one can. I did this to myself. But I won't let him hurt you." Tears were still streaming down her face, even though her voice sounded reasonably coherent.

Forrest sighed, feeling lost. He reached towards her and brushed her cheek with his fingers. *Maintain a prudent distance, Forrest.* But she just wanted to feel protected. She deserved that. For all the confidence she projected, which he loved, she was still so young.

Chapter 14

"Gillian," Forrest said. "You don't need to worry about me."

Addie opened the door to the room, speaking quietly. "Okay, Chinese ordered and on its way. Sorry, had to answer my beeper on my way, but I got it handled, so now we can—oh, Gillian, you're up! And crying . . . Is everything all right?"

Gillian nodded as she smiled. Forrest offered his hand to her.

"She woke up. Guess she wasn't as deeply asleep as I thought," Forrest answered. "Sorry for calling you."

"Oh? Gillian, are you feeling okay?" Addie walked closer to the couch.

"F-fine." Gillian cleared her throat as she took Forrest's hand. He had her up in two seconds. "Sorry, guess my lack of sleep caught up with me." She glanced at Forrest once again. "What time is it?"

"Time for you to go home. Forrest will drive you," Addie said firmly.

"Yes, yes, you must be starving." She chose to ignore Addie's authoritarian tone. "Can we still make it to dinner?" She picked up her quilt and began to fold it. She didn't know how she felt about dinner. She was feeling pretty uncomfortable. Gillian smiled as she cleared her throat again. She had nevertheless invited him, and she wasn't going to be rude.

"No. Dinner will go to your house. You're not going out in your condition," Addie said, interrupting her train of thought.

There was that tone again. Gillian wasn't in the mood for this. She forced herself to remember that Addie was just worried about her. Even if she didn't exactly sound like it right now.

"Condition? I'm fine, just a little restless. I'm sure if Dr. Wolfe is still up for it, we can still go out."

"We already ordered Chinese." Forrest shrugged. "You looked exhausted and I didn't want to wake you, so Addie suggested—I'm fine with it, really. We can go to dinner another time."

"That's nice of you, Dr. Wolfe, but not necessary. I like to keep my commitments."

"Not necessary? Really, Gillian, you've been a walking zombie for the last couple of days, don't think I haven't noticed. I ordered food for *Dr. Wolfe*, too, so you guys can have this discussion after he drives you home," Addie said, still in that tone of voice.

"Oh, well, in that case, I can zoom myself home." Gillian glanced at Addie. "I'll see you there, Dr. Wolfe?"

"Gillian, I brought the Volvo. I don't mind taking you home," Forrest offered, passing his hand through his hair.

Gillian could see he was uneasy. When he was uneasy he didn't know what to do with his hands. And he was pacing. She knew how he felt. Addie tended to have, and was right now having, that effect on her too.

"Thanks, but no need. Besides, you were the one who told me to not stand on my feet for long. I'll see you there." She started walking towards the door.

"All right, that's it."

Gillian knew Addie had been loud on purpose. She thanked the stars she wasn't next to any patient rooms. She knew what Addie wanted and she hated her for putting Forrest in the middle of it, but damn it, she was not in the mood to give her the satisfaction. Not today, not after the day she had had and the nightmares she had woken from. Not when Addie wouldn't take her nightmares seriously, not when she needed to go home and do some serious thinking. And the time it would take Forrest to drive to her place would provide her exactly that if she zoomed.

"Addie, take it easy. If she feels well enough to leave on her own, maybe we should let her."

"Tell me, Gillian, what happened the last time you zoomed exhausted? I know you can zoom everywhere now, I know you have mastered more powers and can now travel wherever you damn please. But your lifeforce still takes a hit, and your exhaustion tonight is obvious," Addie interrupted Forrest.

"Addie, I was seventeen, so let's not go there, okay?"

"Let's see if I remember correctly. You broke your… tibia, was it? I had to cancel all my surgeries because it was the first time that your mother wouldn't be there when you woke up."

"I was angry and I—" Gillian suppressed a sob.

"Yes, you were, and you attempted to do magic when you hadn't slept straight for two weeks."

"I learned my lesson! I had to learn all of them before I was twenty! And not by choice. So, excuse me if I feel confident enough to make my own decisions tonight. And aren't you on call? Gosh, aren't I lucky. Good night!" Gillian huffed, walking away at a faster pace. Her ankle was throbbing, but she was too angry to care anymore, and her tears were clouding her view. Better that she walk away while she still had some measure of control left in her.

"Yes, and Hawkins isn't here, which means someone else would have to stay at your bedside." Addie wouldn't stop. "So, Forrest, how about it?"

"Don't." Gillian turned around.

"What's that?" Addie crossed her arms.

"Don't bring him into this." Gillian started to walk towards her. "He had nothing to do with it."

"With what? You fracturing below your knee? Damn right he didn't. If you weren't so stubborn, the accident could've easily been avoided."

"Addie—" started Forrest.

"Shut up!" Gillian turned to Forrest. This was so typical of him! But today, she wouldn't budge. She'd remained quiet for too long already. "Yes, that's right." Her glance went back to Addie. "But my stubbornness was all your doing."

"Now listen, missy, I still remember telling you—"

"Forrest was sent abroad to save your life. My mother took a huge risk so you could live to go to medical school. And you—you couldn't return the favor. You refused to give her immortality! She should have stuck around. I was only a teenager, Addie!"

Addie's face went from anger to shock. Clearly, she hadn't expected Gillian to bring that topic up. Not now, not ever. Well, good. As far as Gillian was concerned, the topic was long overdue. And Addie had opened the door.

"Oh, shit," she distinctly heard Forrest curse. But now was not the time to linger on the fact that he had never cursed for as long as she had known him, at least not in front of her.

"Gillian, your mother chose to go."

"All the medical education under your belt and you couldn't save the one who mattered most," Gillian said in a low voice.

"She chose not to be bitten, Gillian! There was nothing I could do about it!" Addie went to her.

"Yes, that's right, you vampires and your twisted free-will rules. Well, now it's my turn. I'm choosing to travel how I wish. I lost my mother, Addie, and there's no way in hell you took her place."

Chapter 15

2006

"Mom?"

No answer. Gillian sighed. There was no sight of her anywhere near the nurse's lounge. And she was starving. She hadn't appreciated the choices in the high school's cafeteria today, so she was hoping to borrow her mom for a discounted late lunch. While hospital food was almost as plain as high school food, she could always find more—and usually better—options than either the school or her house's fridge. Ever since her mother had found out that her father was missing, she had been determined to cook all of his favorite foods. She said that when he came back, he deserved a reward for his service, and practice made perfect. And she held out hope that every day would be the day he would find a way back to his family. Suffice to say, the repetition of meals combined with Gillian's picky palate hadn't made for a very satisfied high schooler.

"Mom!" Gillian adjusted the school bag resting on her shoulder. "Oh, Dr. Wolfe, wait up!" Gillian quickened her pace to catch up with the new anesthesiology attending. "Dr. Wolfe!" She made it behind him just in time to catch his conversation with the charge nurse.

"Have Nurse Brystol call me when the patient wakes up. I want to check for any issues with the anesthesia traces," he said.

"Yes, Dr. Wolfe," the white uniformed nurse offered, walking away.

"Dr. Wolfe!"

"Hey, Gillian! How are you?" He smiled as he put his hand on her shoulder.

"Okay." She avoided his gaze, putting a chunk of light blonde hair behind her ear. She hoped he hadn't caught what was sure to be her crimson cheeks. She had to admit the doctor was cute.

"Great," he said again, smiling. "Now, what can I do for you?"

"Any idea where my mom is?" She felt her stomach growl and instinctively put her hand on it. She hoped he hadn't heard that.

"Oh, I'm sure we can find her."

"Dr. Wolfe, a moment of your time, please?" Gillian looked up as her mother's lavender smell reached her nostrils.

"Oh, certainly, Nurse Cassidy. Look who I found!" Forrest put his hand on Gillian's back, pushing her forward.

"Mom, I'm starved. Can we get lunch?"

"Gillian! I have some business to take care with Dr. Wolfe that can't wait, all right?" Gillian detected an urgency in her tone. But she was still hungry.

"When have I heard that before? Come on, Mom! I haven't eaten since this morning."

"What's wrong with the supper I left at the house, Gilly?"

Gillian avoided Forrest's gaze once more. She hated her mother's childish nickname for her, especially when said in front of handsome men.

"Nothing, Mom. I haven't been to the house. I thought, you know, we could spend some time together. You're such a ghost these days and with me going to college soon and all—"

"College? You're fourteen, Gilly. You'll wait a while." Bridget crossed her arms. Gillian knew her mother had seen through her façade. But she didn't want another meal that reminded her of her father. Those were getting tiring, and Martin Joseph Cassidy had not cared much for seasoning. She was sick of plain-tasting meals. Hospital food wasn't that much better, except that it was something out of the ordinary. And she could always find something she liked at least a little bit.

Her mother sighed, her white complexion and cheeks blushing in the hospital's heat, displaying the far-away sadness that had become so natural to her. "Gillian, I really can't right now. But if you just wait in the break room—"

"Tell you what, Gillian, take my card and we'll be right behind you, all right?" Dr. Wolfe chimed in, giving her his ID.

"You really don't have to do that, Dr. Wolfe." Her mother sounded rather mortified. Gillian's face felt hot, once again.

"I insist. Got to get family time when you can, right? My mother always says that, and you're as close

as I get here at the hospital. I could use a snack anyway. Go on, we'll be right behind you. Tell them I sent
you and get whatever you like." Forrest Wolfe smiled
at her again.

"Okay, thanks," Gillian whispered, smiling and
making her way down the hallway.

"What's the matter?" she heard the sandy-blond
doctor whisper behind her.

"It's Adelaide. She's being deployed."

"I thought you told her not to sign up!"

"Because she listens to me so well."

Even walking away, Gillian could hear how upset
her mother was. If only she cared so much about her
own daughter's matters.

"I'll look after her. You have my word."

"I know you will. But there's something else."

Gillian couldn't see what her mother handed
the doctor, but it was probably another one of her
potions that she wouldn't let her help with.

"What is this?" she heard Forrest whisper.

"It's from Gregory Brystol. Call it a life insurance
policy."

"He's a vamp—"

"Shhh! Not in the hallway."

Gillian sighed as she got into the elevator for
the hospital cafeteria. She was sure she would hear
about it this evening. What had her mother done for
Adelaide Brystol this time?

Chapter 16

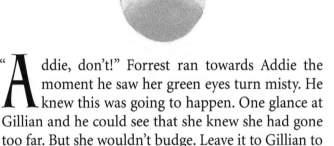

2013

"**A**ddie, don't!" Forrest ran towards Addie the moment he saw her green eyes turn misty. He knew this was going to happen. One glance at Gillian and he could see that she knew she had gone too far. But she wouldn't budge. Leave it to Gillian to be defiant in a moment like this.

Would Addie harm her? He found it unlikely. Gillian was, in the end, like a daughter to her. Nevertheless, vampire rage wouldn't have been infamous if it was easy to control. He wasn't going to take that chance. The fact that Addie was already vamped up hadn't given him a chance to turn into a lycan, not when Gillian had toned down his rage, not when he needed more energy to turn into his animal form when the full moon didn't make its appearance. Damn it.

He wrapped his hands around Addie's abdomen. Hopefully his presence would clear her senses before she could fully transform.

Too late.

Addie turned around and took him by his neck, her predatory misty green eyes and red lips, obscured by her sharp incisors, casting her into an intimidating and beautiful fierce creature. Before he could react, he had collided against the back wall of Gillian's office. He heard a slap and saw Gillian fall to the floor.

His transformation came swiftly, and he positioned himself in wolf form, a gray-haired, four-pawed creature, above Gillian as Addie aimed a kick for her stomach. He wouldn't fight her. He couldn't both do that and protect Gillian. But he did growl at her, hoping that would make Addie aware of what exactly she was putting at risk.

The kick never came. He covered Gillian's face, noticing she was shaking uncontrollably. He heard glass break and felt it pierce his fur. It would heal on its own. But there went Gillian's flower vase, and undoubtedly the flowers he had offered her this morning. Hell of a way for Addie to blow off steam.

"Get her out of here, Forrest," he heard Addie whisper as her eyes went back to their normal green, her incisors shrinking, back to her classically beautiful, impressive frame. "I'm not going to visit tonight after my shift, so you better stay with her." Addie turned on her heel and looked back at him. "Oh, and Forrest, that will bruise. Do something about that, would you? She'll need a prescription for the pain. Demerol should work."

He transformed back just as the door was closing. Gillian's magic had one perk: he transformed back fully clothed. That had been one of his conditions, and she had been able to make it happen.

"All right, Gillian," he whispered. "Up we go."

"No," she whispered, shrinking into a fetal position as she sobbed, still trembling.

"It's okay. It's me. Let's get you home." He put his arms around her, slowly picking her up. She quickly had her arms around him and her face buried in his jacket. At least she wouldn't put up a struggle.

Chapter 17

"Ow! Oh." Gillian squirmed as she felt the cold ice pressing against her already painful cheek. "Easy. Keep a little pressure on this while I go get your prescription," Forrest murmured, which was really nice of him considering her blinding headache at the moment. "Do you want some tea or anything?"

"No, no thanks. And I don't need anything. I feel fine." Gillian sighed as she leaned on her Grandpa's chair. She couldn't wait until Forrest did his work so she could go to bed. It had been hard enough not to fall asleep in the warmed faux-leather seats of his car. Of course, his insistence on keeping his hand pressed with a bag of ice against her face while he drove probably had something to do with that. And to top the night off, she was having trouble understanding herself with the swollen area on the side of her jaw.

Forrest's chuckle told her he was thinking along the same lines.

"Yeah, you say that now, but that's because your mouth is already numb from the ice. Trust me, you'll need it. And it's not advisable to take it on an empty stomach. I'll get you some fruit, or did you want the Chinese food Addie ordered? Okay, no, got it," he added when she couldn't help but gag. "I'll be right back."

Gillian closed her eyes. And then she heard her cell phone ring.

She had never been a phone person, so it seldom rang. After all, almost all her important phone calls were taken at work. All the more reason to get worried. If someone was calling her after nine at night, it was important.

Gillian groaned. Whoever was calling was certainly persistent. The idea of getting up with her head throbbing was just as appealing as eating Chinese right now. Maybe she could move it the magical way. Her blue purse seemed near enough to reach. She groaned once more. Her mother had taught her that she shouldn't do magic if she didn't take care of herself first, both physically and emotionally. After the argument with Addie, and Addie slapping her, magic should have been the last thing on her mind. Except the phone was still ringing.

Her mother had done it. She had done magic under less than ideal circumstances. More than that, she had been able to control Addie's impulses by holding her against the wall magically until she calmed down—one time after her mother had pulled a double shift and once when she had been recovering from a bout of bronchitis.

Gillian should be able to move a silly purse.

Taking a deep breath, she focused as best as she could. Her right hand moved from the armrest. She smiled as she saw the purse start to move toward her. Her head was starting to hurt even more, which she didn't know was possible at this point. It shouldn't have taken very much magic, a circular motion coming from her wrist. She suddenly felt very dizzy, but she could swear it was moving her way. Just one more minute.

"Here you go, Gillian. I—what are you doing? Stop!"

Gillian gasped as she heard the werewolf's voice and the distinct noise of one of her crystal plates breaking on the gray-tiled floor. He looked so blurry as she turned to face him. And the purse looked even blurrier as it hit him in the face. Well, at least it made it. It would have been funny if she hadn't suddenly felt nauseous.

"Ouch, Gillian. Gillian, can you hear me? Damn it."

Her eyes opened briefly as she felt his hands on her face.

"Dr. Wolfe, must you be so loud?" she whispered.

"Didn't your mother tell you not to do magic when you're hurt? Stay with me, you need sugar, and yes, that's what she said." Hilarious. She could hear the thumping of his footsteps as the werewolf hurried into the kitchen.

He hurried back into the room. She felt the palm of his hand touch her cheek, his other hand holding a glass with some orange substance. "Good God, you're freezing! Here, drink this." He lifted her chin.

Gillian choked as she tasted the orange juice. It

wasn't even chilled! "Drink it," the werewolf whispered as he practically forced the drink down her throat. But it did make her feel better. The dizziness went away, but the headache stayed the same. And now, her jaw felt a lot worse.

"Okay, I'm done." Gillian pressed against her jaw while her other hand pushed the glass away. Talking was aggravating her pain right now.

"Fine. Now up we go." Forrest hoisted her up.

"But," Gillian pointed at the phone. Her purse was next to it on the floor, not to mention the plate with grapes, which still lay broken and spilled. She hated to leave messes without cleaning overnight. The grapes could stain the floor if she didn't get to it.

"I'll clean that up and pick up your purse after I've settled you down in your room. Your recovery is more important at this point." Gillian could tell Forrest's voice was restrained. Was he actually mad at her?

"But the phone fell. And it was ringing." Yes, Gillian was aware that she sounded like a child. But with the pain and the stress the night had put on her, thoughts were becoming hard to come by at this point.

"If it's really important, they'll call at a more reasonable hour tomorrow."

"Fine, you're right. It's probably Addie, and I don't want to talk to her anyway," Gillian admitted, more to herself than to him. He heard her and chuckled.

"Okay. The apple doesn't fall far from the tree, I see." Forrest shifted her in his arms as he opened her bedroom door.

"What does that mean?" she couldn't help but huff as he slowly put her on the bed, her cat again hissing as Gillian got settled. But she just cuddled the feline in her arms. Despite the eye roll Dagonet gave to her after looking at the lycan, *sneaky bastard*, and then back at her, he settled down. Good, she wasn't in the mood to fight with both the werewolf *and* the cat. Right now, she needed something to distract her from the pain and dizziness fighting its way through her body.

"It's just, it's funny that you're as stubborn as Addie." He smiled at her as he pulled a chair next to her bed.

"Well, I wouldn't need to be if she treated me like I deserve to be treated." Gillian crossed her arms as she leaned against her pillow, Dagonet now resting by her side, purring as her hand settled on his neck, her nails stroking his fur. *Good kitty.*

"I see," Forrest said, smiling. "And what way is that?"

"Like a colleague, not a child."

"Well, Addie's older than you, and she's immortal. And she feels like she needs to take care of you; she promised your mother after all. I wouldn't be too hard on her. Have you told her this?"

"I've tried," Gillian shrugged. Unfortunately, telling Addie exactly what she thought wasn't easy to do.

"I believe it. Please be more careful next time." Forrest took another bag of ice and pressed it against her face.

"What does that mean? She started it!" Gillian knew she probably sounded like a kid, but the anger she felt earlier was returning in full force now, combined with resentment.

"How long have we been friends with vampires, Gillian?"

"Too long, in my opinion." Gillian let out a deep breath.

"My point exactly. You know they're proud, vain creatures who hate to be proven wrong. And you also know that their strength is nothing to be trifled with, especially if you don't have their same attributes."

"What, you mean immortality? I don't want it. I can take care of myself just fine."

"You don't want it, that's up to you, but don't delude yourself into thinking you've got the upper hand here, especially going after a vampire. You don't. As much as Addie loves you, she has a lot to learn about controlling her rage. So why do we keep going down this same road?"

"What road? Today's the first time that she beat the crap out of me."

"That's true. But you really hurt her. Look, you don't need this right now. You need your rest. But perhaps this will give you something to think about next time you feel in the mood to argue with a creature of the night." Forrest stood up as he pushed the chair back against the wall.

"Fine. I'll think about it later. I've got a long day of work tomorrow."

"Gillian, you're not going to work tomorrow. You're resting."

"I'll be fine."

"No buts. I'll be back in a moment."

"Dr. Wolfe?" Gillian grimaced as she pressed against her jaw in an effort to counterbalance the pain.

"Mm?" Forrest leaned against the door.

"I'm sorry about dinner." And she meant it. He deserved an apology. It was after ten thirty on his night off and he was still being a physician.

"So am I," he whispered, closing the door after himself.

Chapter 18

2008

"Addie, calm down." Forrest put his hands on her shoulders, effectively standing now between her and Bridget's room.

"Forrest, I'm grateful, but if you don't back off right now, I'll be forced to test my new immortality on you." She tried to restrain her voice as much as she could. She didn't want to sound ungrateful to the man who was responsible for her making it home from Afghanistan. But she had to see Bridget.

And she had to give Bridget immortality, even if that went against hospital protocol. Death, after all, was considered natural, inevitable. Immortality wasn't widely known or accepted. She would need a long explanation for Bridget's fortunate, even miraculous, recovery. She would figure it out later. She had a feeling Gillian would never forgive her if she didn't.

"Since you were just born, figuratively speaking, a couple of weeks ago, I doubt that will be a very effective strategy. So for your sake, I'll pretend I didn't hear that. Addie, I need to warn you, Bridget is very sick. She looks nothing at all like you remember her."

"I've seen sick people before, Dr. Wolfe." How dare he? Had they not worked together in Kabul?

"You've seen war wounds, war dead. No one lived long enough to succumb to a sickness. They wouldn't have been in Camp Eggers anyway."

"Could you stop patronizing me and let me in?"

"Let her in, Forrest. It's all right." Both Addie and Forrest went quiet as they heard Bridget's voice.

Forrest extended his hand in front of her. "After you."

Addie scoffed as she went toward the room. Forrest could be so annoying. Bridget wouldn't be sick for long. She'd show him.

"Hello, Adelaide."

Addie should have been cross at being called by her birth name, which she found absolutely detestable and now didn't exist anywhere except on her birth certificate. Well that, and her mother's yearly birthday cards. But everyone else called her Addie. Right now, though, she had bigger problems than being reminded why she came up with her nickname. She stepped into the room.

Addie couldn't help but gasp as she saw her friend and mentor lying in her hospital bed. She looked so yellow, so weak, and hopeless. She steeled herself. "Bridget, how are you feeling?"

"Well, as you can see, I've been better. Thank you for coming, dear." Bridget looked to be struggling just to whisper a few words.

No worries, it wouldn't be for much longer. "Today's your lucky day, Bridge. You'll feel better in no time," Addie whispered back, flipping off the lights.

She heard a tiny gasp from Bridget's bed.

"Addie, we talked about this." Forrest's voice came from behind her.

"Shut up and close the door," she commanded, getting closer to Bridget's bed.

"It worked, didn't it? I mean, I know you told me, but seeing it is—" Bridget whispered, no doubt noticing the dilation of Addie's green eyes, to Forrest.

"Yes, and a little warning would've been nice Bridget, a little choice in the matter," Addie interjected, "But no matter, we can talk about this later. Just so the two of you know though, it hurt worse than the shrapnel."

"I'm sorry, dear, but you'd never have believed me otherwise. If I remember correctly, you once referred to immortality as a *bunch of bullshit*. Weird, coming from a vampire's daughter. Well, weird until I discovered that your mother didn't want you to know. Poor Dorothy always felt ashamed about what happened and I—"

"Yes, Bridget, I know. We don't have a lot of time. You can finish filling in the details of what Forrest told me later, as unpleasant as that was." She wasn't in the mood to discuss it now, not when Bridget needed what she herself had refused to believe existed, let alone worked.

And that which she now had, thanks in large part to her blond friend behind her.

"No time? Is there somewhere you need to be?" Bridget looked puzzled.

Her friend must be sicker than she thought. Did she honestly think she wouldn't return the favor?

"Well, no. But after we're done, you'll be asleep for some time. We can discuss everything when you feel better and are on your feet again. Forrest, I told you to close the door!"

"Addie, I told you she doesn't want it." Forrest tried to interfere once more.

Addie wouldn't have it. "Shut up and do as I tell you. I'll be the judge of that." Addie noticed Bridget's distressed demeanor. *Well, that can't be good.* "Oh Bridget, are you okay?"

"Forrest is right. I don't want it," her mentor confirmed.

Addie had heard it from Forrest, had seen her friend's anguished face, but she still couldn't believe what she was hearing. Who *wouldn't* want it? She had a daughter, for crying out loud! And she was Addie's mentor.

"Bridget, that's nonsense. You're ill. I'll make you feel better."

"I said no, Adelaide. You're new, but I'm sure Forrest has already filled you in on the rules regarding free will."

Bridget's tone made her back away from the bed. Bridget might be mortal and sick, but her formidable powers made Addie hesitate. She could be a mean witch when she was angry.

"Bridget, you don't mean that. What about Gillian?"

"Gillian will understand in time."

"She will? How? Because I sure don't!"

"Keep your voice down!" Forrest whispered.

"It's the vampire in her, Forrest," Bridget said

calmly. "Let her get it out. In time, she'll learn to control it."

"Not without you I won't!"

"You'll understand in time, too, dear."

"You're jaundiced, Bridget. And you're spouting utter nonsense! Let me fix it!"

"No, Adelaide. Immortality can't fix everything. It cannot be allowed to. Life goes on. We have to keep the balance."

"Shit, Bridget, *you* gave it to me!"

"No. Your father did, by giving your mother his blood, in case a time came that she needed it. But he let her be the judge. Giving a life carries a risk, after all. Your mother came to me. You know we go way back to nursing school. You barely talk to her, so she knew you wouldn't let her convince you not to enlist, you being so stubborn. I accepted the responsibility to pass it to someone who would make sure you'd survive your time in the war, since you insisted on enlisting, despite my reluctance. I'm very grateful to Dr. Wolfe, who accepted the risk and responsibility to smuggle it across the front lines and keep his eye on you, if only for friendship's sake, since he insists he doesn't care about the debt you owe him for turning you, despite your immortal enmity by virtue of your separate species. How can I ever repay you, young man?"

"Why give it to me if I can't use it to save you?"

"You're such a good doctor—a young doctor, Addie. There are so many things you'll do. So many experiences worth living. I couldn't let the war take that away from you. Not when so many patients need you."

"And they don't need you? For heaven's sake, Bridge, you're in that bed because of them."

"I'm a nurse. I knew the risks. Disease is not evil, Adelaide. It restores balance to the life and death equation."

"Well, good luck telling Gillian that pile of cow dung."

"I tried to. That will fall to you now."

"Pardon?" Now that she didn't expect.

"Gillian is young and impulsive. I need you to take care of her, help her to develop her powers by being there for her. I don't trust the coven to carry out this responsibility. She has to learn the rules on her own. Too much power scares other older, witches, not to mention the danger of concentrating power in one place. Individual magic is lonely perhaps, but safe. Be there for her, like she'll be there for you. Help her to continue my legacy. One day . . ." Bridget struggled to take another breath.

"Bridget!" Addie rushed back to her bedside.

Bridget put her hand up, stopping her in her tracks. "Please. One day she'll understand how important her magic is. Please."

Addie watched her friend struggle not to cry. She felt Forrest rest his hand on her shoulder.

"Please let her know how much I love her, Adelaide. I'm so proud of her. And I'm sorry I can't watch her grow up."

"But you can, Bridget. I can make you immortal."

"No, Adelaide, my time is up. I accept that. Please, promise me you'll take care of my girl."

"Bridget—"

"Please, so I can go in peace."

Addie couldn't stand her friend begging. She felt like she might crumble into a million pieces. Even if she was immortal, the newness of it still made her body fragile.

She nodded.

"Thank you, Adelaide." With a sigh, Bridget closed her eyes.

"Doctor!" Addie tried to launch at Bridget as her heart monitor flatlined.

"Addie, no! This is what she wants! Let her go!" Forrest grabbed her waist, preventing her from getting to the bed.

"Let go, werewolf, or I swear—"

"She wants to go! She's a nurse, Addie, she understands. Let her go. She did so much for you, so grant her that last wish. Addie, please."

Forrest's pleas pulled all the energy out of her. Her tears became full-on sobs as she withdrew all her resistance and rested in Forrest arms. He pulled her to him.

"Mom?" Gillian's small voice felt like an echo to Addie's ears.

Chapter 19

2013

"You look like hell." Addie's brows furrowed as she put her red Corvette's keys on the kitchen counter along with her green mug.

"Did you honestly think I would have a good night's sleep?" Forrest grumbled as he sipped his cup of coffee. Raw bacon was sitting on a plate at his side, but she could tell he hadn't touched it.

"The medication should've knocked Gillian out, at least," Addie said as she made her way to the blood fridge, a black, small one sitting opposite the white food fridge.

"It did," Forrest whispered. "And lower your voice. She hasn't gotten up yet."

"Jeez, Forrest, I can smell the caffeine from over here," Addie huffed. As a young woman, she had never grown to appreciate coffee. Suffice it to say that now, on a straight blood diet, things hadn't changed.

"You're about to feed, which means your senses are enhanced. And how else do you suppose I'd stay awake today?"

"Do you have to go in?" Addie took her cup, sitting down with him.

Forrest nodded. "I thought that's why you were here."

"I wasn't sure. I just got out." Addie took a drink as Forrest sighed. "Okay, what's going on?"

Forrest raised his eyebrows, still sleepy. "What do you mean?"

"Was it Gillian? Did she take it out on you?" Forrest was immortal; he had had a long time to get used to the medical profession. Bouts of insomnia weren't usual for him unless something was really getting under his skin.

"Gillian's general impulsiveness hasn't bothered me before." Forrest shrugged, but didn't glance at her. He seemed to be deep in thought. "This time it was dangerous, though, her doing magic. She almost fainted trying to levitate the purse to get to the phone."

"She did *what*?"

"Keep your voice down!"

"Oh, so she can ruin your night, but she can't lose one ounce of beauty sleep?" Addie stood up, unable to hide her anger any longer.

"She didn't ruin my night, Addie, you did," Forrest whispered.

"That's not true!"

"Oh, isn't it?" Forrest's sarcastic remark was as close as he got to being mad. That meant he wasn't letting this go.

"She provoked me!" Addie realized in the back of her mind that her accusatory tone didn't sound mature. She had been working hard to control her rage. The fact that she could so easily be provoked both embarrassed and enraged her even more.

"That she did. But you started it," Forrest pointed out.

"Oh, come off it, Forrest. Since when is it a crime to worry?"

"I'm not saying it is. But you made it sound like she had no choice but to do what you said."

"She could've gotten hurt!"

"Oh, you mean she didn't?" There was that sarcastic tone again.

Addie sat back down. If she didn't calm down soon, she was going to punch something, or someone. And she didn't want to punch Forrest.

"So there was a little pain. She can deal with it."

"Can *you*?"

"What do you want me to say? I'm sorry? I am, for hitting her. But everything I said was true. And it is so easy for you to say!"

"Why? Because I don't have a promise to her mother hanging over my head? Don't make it sound like I don't care about her, Addie, because that couldn't be further from the truth and you know it. That independence, that selflessness, I've never seen anything like that woman. And I've been on this earth a long time."

"You don't understand! She's right. I failed. She's always going to see me as the person who, for all intents and purposes, killed her mother! You heard her!"

"She was angry," Forrest whispered, gathering his vampire friend into his arms. She was grateful for his embrace. "She didn't mean it."

"Didn't she?" Addie couldn't help but tear up. Damn it, any thought of Bridget could make her do that.

"Gillian knows you couldn't save her mother. It's just easier in a moment of anger to blame someone."

"Ouch! Damn it! I'm late!" Addie hadn't even opened her mouth to answer when she heard Gillian's voice. She glanced at Forrest.

"Didn't you tell her she can't be going to work today?"

Forrest nodded. "I'd better get her."

"I'll go. Get to the hospital. I'll see you when you're done."

"You sure?"

"Have to face her sooner or later."

"All right, see you." Forrest stood up and put his coffee cup in the sink and the untouched bacon back in the fridge, the white one.

"And Forrest?"

"Yeah?" Forrest turned to face her as he grabbed his brown jacket.

"Thanks." She smiled. Good friends like him were hard to come by.

Chapter 20

"No, Forrest, she can do that when she feels better . . . No, you don't need to come back, I'll handle it . . . Forrest, just go to work . . . Yeah, you have a good one too. Bye."

Addie put her cell phone back in her pocket and made her way to Gillian's room on the second floor. Forrest's affection for the witch was cute, but sometimes she couldn't help but think he took it too far. Did Gillian know how head over heels the lycan was for her? What would Gillian do if she knew? That was the key. Addie knew how Forrest felt. She didn't doubt his feelings. But Gillian . . . Gillian hadn't had a stable relationship—if she could call it that—since she had broken up with, or more accurately, cut off all communication with, Sean Kennard. How open would she be to a new relationship, one with an immortal? Someone she had known since her teenage years, someone her mother had trusted to give Addie a new life?

This was too complicated to face now that she hadn't slept in thirty-six hours. Better take care of the present for the moment.

"I have to go," Gillian said hurriedly after opening the door milliseconds after Addie touched her knuckle to the knob. She still looked a little dazed, Addie noticed.

"I don't think so. Back to bed we go." Addie tried to put some of Gillian's weight against her.

"Addie, I'm late for work."

"You don't have to go in. I've already spoken to Ed."

"Yes, I do. I have work to catch up on!"

"Look at you, Gillian. You can barely stand. I think the hospital will survive without you for one day. From what Forrest told me, your condition last night—"

"Yeah, well, Dr. Wolfe says many things that I have yet to make sense of."

Addie looked into her eyes. It seemed, if that was possible, Gillian was mad at Forrest. Had something happened last night? Was that why Forrest looked miserable this morning?

"Such as?" Addie asked quietly.

"It's not important. What did Ed say?" Gillian walked away, supporting herself on her bedside table to get back into bed. Addie wondered when Gillian had last eaten. And why was she avoiding the subject?

"To come back when you feel better."

"I feel fine!"

"How about going back when you actually *do* feel better. Stop pretending you do." For someone who wanted to be treated like an adult, Gillian sure wasn't acting like one. "Your face may look better, but you're still dizzy. What did you eat last night?"

"Orange juice. And most people don't have to take Demerol when they get their face slapped."

Addie sighed. Gillian was looking for an apology. And as sorry as Addie was that things had gotten out of control, she wasn't sure that Gillian deserved one, not without understanding the point that she was trying to make in the first place.

"You know better than to attempt magic when you're not getting rest, Gillian," she said softly.

"What do you think you asked me to do when I was getting Dr. Wolfe out of the janitor's closet barely two days ago?"

"Okay. That was different, and I did apologize for that."

"Besides, Mom could've done it with her eyes closed even when she was dying with hepatitis."

Oh, how Addie wished she had more experience with teenagers. Gillian was twenty and still she grieved like her sixteen-year-old self. "Your mother was pushing forty. She wasn't better than you, just more experienced. Can't you see that? If I know something, it's that your mother wouldn't have wanted you to push yourself so hard. Almost fainting?"

"Yeah, well, my mother wasn't supposed to leave me when I was sixteen either. All that magic, all the good she had done . . ." Gillian's back pushed the pillow farther into the bed frame as she tried to hold back her tears. Dagonet, bothered by the sudden movement, settled on the other side of the bed, scoffing at Addie in the process.

Addie knew Gillian didn't want to cry in front of

her. How to handle this? She cursed under her breath. Forrest was better at these situations than she had ever been. She supposed her own childlessness, and having grown up with a single mother, was to blame somehow for not knowing how to treat Gillian like the child she had been when her mother had passed. And she had been as hurt as Gillian, mainly because Gillian's mother had refused to live—had refused the offer of immortality. But Gillian had had her own issues to deal with. Her mother had just been taken away from her. Her father had been deployed to Afghanistan and had never come back. When her mother had passed on, Gillian had gone into her own world. She had refused to see a counselor and retreated further and further, practicing magic inside her room.

Addie had confronted her. After all, how many broken bones would she have to mend before Gillian came to her senses and slowed down? Oh, Gillian had had an answer for that too. It was the only thing that made her feel close to her mother. How was she supposed to argue with that? She supposed she should blame Gillian's mother for being selfish. After all, she knew that if she was gone, Gillian would have no one.

That's why she asked me to take care of her.

But Gillian hadn't seen it that way. She had grown up before she was ever supposed to. And now, when she was allowing herself to open a little bit about her grief, Addie didn't have the heart to blame her for her temper tantrums, not when Gillian never had them when she was in public. Not when it was obvious that Gillian felt most vulnerable when her magic wasn't working. Not when Gillian felt she was somehow failing her mother by not being able to keep up with what she thought her mother would have been able to do at her age. Whether her mother could actually do it or not, neither Addie nor Gillian would ever know. But she couldn't blame Gillian for idolizing her.

"I'm sorry, Gillian," Addie said, sitting on the corner of her bed. "I'm sorry she chose to leave you, because I know that's the way you look at it. But she must have had a good reason to decline. And she probably hoped one day you could understand."

"Right." Addie caught Gillian hurriedly wiping away her tears.

"Come here." Addie put her arms around her. For once, Gillian didn't fight her off. "I wish you would talk to me about these things before you actually can't hold it anymore."

"Mm."

"Gillian, I *am* sorry. You could have seriously gotten hurt. If Forrest hadn't been there—"

"I would've been fine.

"Gillian—"

"Addie, my mother trusted you. Why shouldn't I?"

"After what you said last night, I'm not so sure you do. Gill, I am sorry I couldn't save her."

"Oh, Addie, I shouldn't have said that. I shouldn't have blamed you. That wasn't your job, it was hers." Gillian pulled away, sniffling.

"She did make sure you'd be taken care of, Gillian."

"Not by her."

"I don't expect you to understand her choice. But look at you. You've expressed, multiple times, both to Forrest and to me, that you don't want to be immortal. Why not?"

"It brings more problems than it solves. It's that

simple," Gillian whispered, clearly uncomfortable with the subject.

"You're basing this on Sean, aren't you? One mistake," Addie pointed out, though she was sure that Gillian didn't want to hear it.

"With consequences that will last many lifetimes. Great job me."

"Is that it? If you were about to die and I offered immortality, would you reject it because of Sean?"

"I just want to see her, Addie. I'd give anything for that, for an explanation, for closure."

"Your mother used to contact a variety of people in other dimensions. Would that do it?"

"Don't you think I've tried that? She doesn't want to see me."

"I'm sure that's not the case. She would give anything to see you, I bet."

"When you open up a portal, the other person has to willingly come out. I've spent hours waiting." Addie put her hand on Gillian's shoulder as she saw her starting to tear up once more.

"Well, I'm sure she has a good explanation for it."

"Yeah, so do I."

"No, Gillian, that's not what I meant."

"How long do I have to stay locked up here?" Gillian suddenly asked, leaning against her pillow again.

Addie pursed her lips. She wouldn't protest. She wouldn't force the topic any further. "Let's see how you fare today. We'll keep an eye on you and then we'll decide."

"Is Dr. Wolfe coming back?" Gillian shifted against her pillows, taking one teddy bear to hug now that her cat still refused to move across from Addie. Addie raised her eyebrows. Gillian had looked exceedingly uncomfortable today every time Forrest was brought up

"I'm working tonight again, Gillian. I don't mean to pry, but is there something going on with you two? Did you have a fight or something?"

"It's fine, Addie. Just a question." Gillian shrugged it off. "I just feel bad about dinner is all."

"I'm sure he understands, Gillian."

"Just because he's too nice to protest, Addie, doesn't mean he's okay with it."

"Well, I happen to know he has no problem with this assignment." Addie smiled, but Gillian didn't appear to be comforted. In fact, she looked even more uncomfortable. "Gillian, are you all right? Do you prefer I stay?"

"No. Go to work. I would if I could."

"I know you've been stressing out. And I'm sure your nightmares don't help. But Sean can't hurt you anymore, or anyone close to you, for that matter."

Gillian sighed, but just smiled, taking Dagonet back into her arms after forcing him out of his sitting position. *Too bad, I want to cuddle.*

Addie sounded so sure of that fact. But based on the past couple of days, Gillian couldn't agree.

Chapter 21

2008

"Sean," Gillian gasped. "What are you doing here?" She sighed, hastily cleaning her tears as she watched her once-warm breath come out of her mouth. It was a chilly November night, with a clear sky. That was a rare sight in the late fall for the normally snow-covered city, and Gillian had taken advantage of the starry sky to clear her head.

"You weren't at our usual spot," Sean complained, referring to the woody patch of land at the back of the high school.

"That's because you're not supposed to be out and about, Sean. Oh . . . did you go through with it?" Gillian whispered.

"Check it out." Sean sat by her side and Gillian spotted the misty quality of vampire eyes reflected in his dark brown gaze. He looked paler than usual as he moved under the porch's light.

She backed away. "It worked," Gillian whispered, her wonder masking the fear, fear that it would hurt, fear that she would never be the same. But her mother would be saved. And she would get to be with Sean forever. That was worth a little pain and fear.

"Yeah, your guy Callahan came through. It wasn't even that bad, really. Just wished we could've done it together is all."

"I know Sean, I'm sorry. They thought they had found a liver for my Mom. It wasn't a match, but I had to be there for her, just in case. I'm glad Callahan came through, for what we paid him."

"Small price to pay for immortality, babe. And after tomorrow, you won't have to worry about a possible liver for your mom." Sean flashed her a cocky smile, standing once again.

Gillian noticed Sean wasn't wearing a coat, and as he smiled, his incisors were displayed in their full, intimidating force. But in his T-shirt and jeans, Sean looked comfortable with the chilly weather. Figured, as vampires did not have the burden of body temperature to worry about.

"Did you feed? How are you feeling?"

"A little light-headed, but Callahan said it'll pass."

"Callahan also said you should be resting." Gillian gave him what she hoped was a stern look. As a new vampire, he would be weak for quite some time, at least until his body got used to the change. That meant minimal, if any, sunlight exposure (though Gillian doubted that would be a problem in normally dreary Erie), and plenty of rest. One down, one to go.

"I couldn't miss the opportunity to see my hot mortal girl one last time." He winked at her.

"I'll still be the same, Sean, just a little colder."
Gillian shrugged. She was really trying to make the
matter seem trivial. It should have been. After all, her
friends were immortal. How bad could it be? Addie
and Forrest certainly didn't seem to have any complaints. But the truth was, she couldn't escape the fear
that gripped her insides.

This is for you, Mom.

Her mother was going to live. She was going to be
there in case her father came back. She was going to be
there to see her graduate from high school, to become
a full-fledged, immortal witch. Even though she had
never heard of one. Well, she would be the first one,
then. Her powers wouldn't be affected, would they?
After all, she had been born with her magic, like she
had been born with silvery blond hair. Those genetic
traits didn't go away simply because of immortality,
did they? These thoughts, though not completely
sorted out, were what kept her going. Screw Addie,
what did she know? She would save her mother. And
at the end of the day, Addie would both be sorry she
didn't do it and thankful that Gillian had managed to
keep her mentor alive. And her mother—well, hopefully she would be proud of her initiative.

"Well, yeah, but immortal. I just thought we
should celebrate your last night as a mortal, and
my first one as an immortal." He sat down with her
again. With the porch light reflecting indirectly on
him, he didn't look as intimidating. This was Sean,
the love of her life. He would never harm her, and
despite that sometimes nasty temper of his, he loved
her. Wasn't that the truth? Did he love her as much
as she loved him?

"What did you have in mind?" Gillian whispered as Sean's mouth curled softly into a smile.

"Oh," Sean whispered, cupping her cheek with his hand and making Gillian tremble from his cool touch. "Just a night you'll never forget," he finished as he touched her lips with his own.

Their breathy kiss quickly turned more passionate as Sean got closer to her, his teasing tongue opening her mouth.

Gillian let out a gasp as Sean's lips moved to her neck.

"Ouch!" Gillian gasped again as she felt Sean lightly bite her neck.

"That's it," he whispered as he nuzzled her. "You belong to me now."

Chapter 22

2013

"Gillian. Gillian, wake up!"

Gillian gasped as she found herself face-to-face with Forrest's beautiful but intimidating gray eyes. It took her a minute to get used to her room's dark surroundings. The cinnamon smell emanating from her mother's enchanted candle was always a reminder of her whereabouts, and it always served to ground her when she felt overwhelmed. Unfortunately, she couldn't focus on it enough to calm down right now, when one question kept pounding in her head.

What was he doing here?

Why did she keep focusing on his lips?

And where was Dagonet? Why wasn't he hissing right now? She could've used a warning at least.

"Dr. Wolfe," she said, trying to get herself to fully wake up. She could feel his breath on her lips. Her voice felt rough with sleep.

"Gillian, are you all right?"

She brushed her hair back and realized her face was drenched with sweat.

"What's going on?" Well, not as diplomatic as she usually tried to be, but it sure beat *What the hell are you doing here?*

"You were having another nightmare. Did you know you talk in your sleep?" He smiled. Or at least she could discern an attempt at it now that her eyes had adjusted somewhat to the darkness. It had to be after midnight, and he seemed ready to tackle another day. Well, she guessed it was already another day, albeit a tinge too early to tackle, in her opinion.

"You heard me all the way in the basement?" Now she was definitely mortified.

"I was in the living room. But I'm sure you're familiar with lycan hearing." He smiled again.

"Of course." Being with immortals could be exhausting sometimes. "Well, I apologize for waking you up, Dr. Wolfe. I'm fine . . . really. You can go back to sleep now."

"Are you sure? That's three nightmares just this week. And by the look of you, your body isn't happy about the lack of sleep. Want to talk about it?"

"That's really not necessary, Dr. Wolfe. I can handle it myself."

"You always could, Gillian. I don't doubt that. But sometimes we could all use an outsider's perspective."

"The last thing I need is immortality's perspective tonight," she blurted out.

She instantly regretted it as Forrest headed for the

door. "I apologize, Dr. Wolfe, I didn't mean it like that. I appreciate your concern. But this is something I need to deal with on my own."

"You know, Gillian," Forrest turned back and sat at the edge of the bed this time, "there's nothing wrong with asking for help, even for someone with magical powers."

"Oh, trust me, Dr. Wolfe, even magic couldn't fix this."

Forrest lifted his hands in the air. She knew he meant well.

If you only knew what I did.

"Okay," he said. "Just know I'm here if you change your mind."

"Thank you, Dr. Wolfe." Gillian leaned against the pillow. "It's so much easier to talk to you than to Addie."

"Oh? How so?"

"Well, she insists on treating me like a child," she said before she could stop herself.

"Gillian." The werewolf sat farther onto the baby blue quilt. "She only wants what's best for you. I know she can be annoying sometimes, but given what you've been through, she just doesn't want— well, she wants you to live like you deserve. I gifted her with immortality when she was close to your age. I think you remind her a lot of herself. And then you losing your mother, and her losing her friend and mentor—she knows you went through a lot. And wants to protect you. That's the promise she made to your mother. I'll tell you, if I wasn't immortal, she would treat me like a child. In fact, she often does."

"I know. I want to understand, I do, but . . . well, you're immortal and you don't treat me like a child." There, that's what she had meant to say.

"Yes, that's interesting, isn't it?" His laugh left her puzzled as she suddenly found him looking at the floor.

Was it something I said? "Wait, that was supposed to be a compliment. What did I say?" And she genuinely was puzzled as she found him either unable or unwilling to keep eye contact with her. For the normally confident Dr. Forrest Wolfe, this wasn't good. But what had she done wrong? How could she apologize if she didn't know what she was apologizing for?

"Nothing, nothing that wasn't true. Addie is your guardian, Gillian. I'm, well, not."

"But you were there also. You are with us, all the time."

"Well, because I care about you. Would you prefer I wasn't? Would you prefer I leave?" Forrest looked tense. Why didn't he simply say what he meant? He shouldn't need diplomacy in front of her. They had known each other long enough.

"No! I mean, I'm used to it." Gillian shrugged. He looked . . . even more disappointed. "That sounded much better in my—I didn't mean it the way it sounded, Dr. Wolfe. I'm grateful."

"Yes, well, you're welcome. Tell you what, I'll just say good night and I'll see you tomorrow." He got up and walked towards the door.

"Dr. Wolfe, I—no—wait . . ."

With a grunt, Gillian got out of bed and tried to follow him out of the room. She had to take hold of the bed pillar once she realized how dizzy she felt.

She wiped cold sweat from her forehead. *I really must look like shit.* But the mere thought of walking to her dresser mirror gave her a bigger headache. She had to know what he meant though, what he wanted from her. Her good night's sleep depended on it. And since he had brought it up . . .

"Forrest, um, Dr. Wolfe, wait!"

He probably was in the basement already, locked in his cage. After all, for an upset werewolf—and he *had* looked upset when he left the room—it would be only too easy to transform. He didn't need the full moon. Once he had control of the virus, and Forrest had had a long time to get used to it having been born with it and all, he could transform at will. Anger would only provide an easy excuse to do so.

Running sounded better than walking at this point. The less time she spent standing and the quicker she could be back in bed, the better. Her headache was bad. Taking a deep breath and putting her terry bathrobe on, her hands trying to tame her blond locks as much as her fingers could, she opened her bedroom door. Already with her mind set on running, her legs took on a velocity of their own.

To her horror, she found that Forrest was not in the basement, not even downstairs pondering if the basement would be the alternative for tonight, but sitting at the top of the stairs, his head in his hands.

She didn't have time to stop. Luckily for her, lycans possessed remarkable coordination skills among their many abilities. And Forrest was able to catch her as she toppled over him. He held her against him until they were both able to catch their breath.

"Are you all right?" Forrest whispered, and Gillian had to admit it felt nice.

"I just wanted to . . . I'm sorry," she said, looking up into his gray eyes. They were even more intimidating up close.

"It's fine. But you still haven't answered my question," he said while he examined her.

"I'm all right. But stop treating me like a fool, would you? You've been there, always, with Addie and me. So I know you. And I know that I got under your skin somehow."

"Gillian," Forrest sighed, taking a deep breath, and helped her sit beside him on the stairs.

"Is it Addie? Because I won't say anything. Your secret is safe with me. And who's to say she doesn't see you the same way?"

Now it was the werewolf who looked puzzled, and bemused, if his laughter was any indication.

"Is that what you think? I'm into Addie?"

"Well, aren't you? Not that I blame you, you've been friends a long time. She's a vampire, I get it, the species pact, but you know, she might feel the same towards you. You've been through a lot together after all."

"This isn't about Addie, Gillian." He was still smiling, but there was a healthy blush in his cheeks.

"No need to be embarrassed. Letting her feed off you, that takes guts and I'm sure there were emotions playing there also—"

Suddenly, Gillian realized she couldn't talk, as she felt Forrest's lips on hers.

Well. She supposed that was one way to clarify the situation.

Chapter 23

Forrest's eyes opened slowly as he realized he had massive neck pain. Since Addie was currently occupying his sleeping bag, he had no choice but sit on the floor.

The hours had led him to close his eyes in exhaustion, only to wake up as Addie's moans filled the small space.

Was she in pain?

She wasn't supposed to be. In fact, she was supposed to be dead. Well... undead.

"Adelaide?" He crawled to her side.

Had he even asked Bridget what the consequences of this maneuver would be? Yes, she would live. But at what cost? He had heard from his parents that vampires lost at least a bit of their former selves during the transformation. How much would Addie lose? And would she notice? Would her friends notice?

Was this a one-way ticket to the psych ward? Well, definitely not what Bridget had in mind, he was sure of that.

Forrest sighed as his hand wiped the sweat from his forehead. He now wished he had taken more time to think about this, to focus on what kind of immortal life Addie would have before accepting blindly that he was to save her life and get her back to Erie when her time at the front was over.

"Addie," he tried again. Her eyes were opened, but she seemed to be staring . . . nowhere.

"Uh? What? Who is that?" Addie seemed to be unable to focus for the time being, so he crawled until he was directly in her eyesight. His knees made the tent dig into the sand, and he could feel the earth's scorching heat as the sun beat mercilessly in the early afternoon.

He was lucky no one had disturbed him. Either they were still busy with the Humvee victims or—

He didn't want to think they suspected unconventional methods. But he knew this had been a risk. One that Addie wasn't sure to survive.

And one that could cost him his military career and, in the end, if he wasn't careful, his medical license as well.

Although the United States had become a much more secular country than it was when he was born in 1915, immortality was still thought to be a myth, the devil's work, as God alone had control of a soul coming and going on this earth. Well, as far as he was concerned, those that were born into lycanthropy had as much of a purpose as those mortal-born, or so his Christian mother, Margaret, had told him time and time again. After all, he was born from two lycan parents, so they could not claim ignorance of their son's destiny, to hide in plain sight while leading as normal a life as he possibly could. And although lycans and vampires didn't see exactly eye to eye, his parents had accepted that those former mortals that had survived the poison seeping through their veins still had purpose to fulfill in this world. And so, Addie's work, and his, was far from over. Now that he had used Bridget's insurance policy he would have to live with the consequences. And that meant driving all suspicion away from her, onto himself if need be. Yes, she was alive, but as a newborn vampire, she would be in a weakened state for weeks, if not months, as her body got used to this new way of life. And once she was strong enough to fend for herself, she would need guidance navigating an immortal life. And he doubted her father, the poisoned blood donor, who had been out of her life after getting her mother pregnant, would suddenly volunteer to guide her. So, him, a lycan, would have to do.

"Adelaide? Can you see me?" he whispered once he was in her direct line of sight.

Her normally dark green eyes were light and misty, her frowning face pale, and she squinted several times before she opened her mouth.

"Forrest? What are you doing? What's going on?"

The werewolf sighed in relief. There was sight, and recognition. At this moment of uncertainty, he took the little moments of progress however he could get them.

He sighed. Well, better to get this over with sooner rather than later.

"Well, you're alive for one thing." He shrugged, and an awkward laugh, one of victory over a semi-medical procedure gone right, couldn't help but escape his mouth.

Her face of genuine puzzlement tugged at his heartstrings. Would she understand his reasons? Bridget's? Would she accept her new immortal life?

"What does that mean? Aren't I supposed to be? Ugh! Did a truck run me over?"

"Close. Your convoy caught a grenade. You're lucky to be alive. Well, no, that's not exactly right. Are you hungry?"

"Actually, I am. But I feel like . . . I can't move."

"You'll feel better after you drink this," Forrest sighed, taking a steel thermos out of his med pack. "I kept it cold with dry ice. I'm lucky I still have friends who work in research."

"Thanks, Forrest, but you know I hate coffee. How is cold coffee any different?"

"It's . . . not coffee Addie." Forrest sighed once more, getting the thermos closer to her. Could she hold it steadily? So soon?

"What do you mean? What exactly is it?"

"Call it medication."

"For what?"

"Your . . . condition."

"What do you mean? I happen to have a very good immune system—"

"Probably that's how you survived."

"Survived what? What the hell are you giving me? I'm a fucking nurse for crying out loud—"

Forrest gasped as Addie grasped the thermos from his hand, opening it abruptly. As a consequence, blood splashed on her hands, making her jump, the liquid spilling into her legs.

"Careful! You need that, and I've only got a tight

supply." Forrest pressed his lips together as he saw the look of despair in Addie's eyes. "I'm sorry, but you need to drink it. It's the only way I can keep you alive."

"No," Addie whispered. "No . . . I should've died."

"Your parents wanted you to live, Addie. They gave the blood to Bridget. She . . . she gave it to me."

"And where the hell would they get their hands on vampire blood, Wolfe?"

"From your father, Gregory Brystol, Addie. He's immortal."

"But . . . he's dead. How can he—"

"He's undead, Addie. He just never told you. And your mother didn't bother to correct you when you assumed he was dead simply because he wasn't coming home. He is a vampire, which means the blood of the living keeps his body, and all its systems, alive. It is possible for vampires to procreate—complicated, but possible. One of the partners has to be mortal though. Your mother was it in this case. It is easier for male vampires to create other vampires because mortals carry their child. The child is mortal, if it's born, because a mortal will carry it and its immune system will get rid of the vampire trace. It makes the mother severely weak, and the birth complicated, but it's not unheard of. With a female vampire, well, similar dynamics, as the mortal father's half of the DNA will trump the trace, and blood will keep the mother alive and able to feed nutrients to the baby. Again, complicated, but not unheard of."

"You . . . you did this?" Addie asked, her hand motioning up and down her body. Forrest breathed out. How long before she could say the word? How long before she could accept her own immortality?

"I did, Addie. If you want to be mad, be mad at me. But you're alive. Bridget wanted you to live."

"This . . . isn't a life. You said it yourself, I'm undead!" Addie struggled to get out of the sleeping bag. Her attempt was met with futility. "Let me out!"

"You're still too weak. The sunlight will kill you."

"Let it!" She kept struggling. "My friends were in that Humvee, and you didn't save any of them, did you? I would've given my life for any one of them."

Forrest put his arms around her. Even though her struggles weren't working, that didn't mean she was likely to give up. She was weak right now, as her body adjusted to her new way of life. She had to rest.

"And they would've done the same for you. Bridget chose you. Your father chose you."

"My father left! It was easier to believe he was dead when my mother said it, but I found his letters, and the stupid late-night phone calls when mother would insist someone dialed a wrong number—too many to be a coincidence. He's still dead to me. What gives him the right—let go!"

"You're alive, and whole."

"Oh, is that a fact? 'Cause I sure don't feel my heart beating!"

"Your legs were out of your body, Addie. If you survived the blood loss and the damage, you wouldn't be whole. My job is to try to save you . . . to the best of my ability."

"No, your job is to do no harm!"

"And no harm will come to you. I'll stake my career on it. You'll get back home, get into med school. There's so much good you can do. Think of immortality as what it is in this case—a gift, from your mentor."

Chapter 24

2013

Forrest stirred as he heard a ringing noise next to his pillow on his makeshift bed.

"Shit." He cleared his throat, rubbing sleep away from his eyes as he proceeded to answer his cell phone. He wasn't on call today, thank goodness. He doubted he could stay awake on the mighty two hours of sleep he had gotten last night. However, he had Gillian duty all day. He and Addie had decided that yesterday.

Well, a lot of things had happened yesterday. Without hesitation, he knew who was at the other end of the line. In fact, he was surprised she hadn't called earlier.

"Dr. Wolfe," he answered automatically. He could go with the excuse that he hadn't had his coffee yet. But then again, the way his mind was going over the events with Gillian last night, he doubted he needed the caffeine, at least for the time being.

"Hey, Forrest, how's the patient?"

"What?

"Gillian, Forrest," Forrest heard Addie huff over the phone. "What? She didn't let you sleep again? Oh, that girl."

Forrest sighed, almost in a whispered laugh. He wondered if he should tell her that Gillian was only indirectly responsible. It had been his fault to begin with. What had he been thinking? Although Gillian hadn't complained. In fact, she hadn't said much after they had broken away from the kiss. Neither of them had. Talk about a smooth ending.

"Oh, no. She—"

"Here. Gimme." Gillian took the phone from his hand, droplets from her wet hair prickling his chest as she removed her hair from her face. Well, at least her sleep, judging by the fact she'd had time for a shower, couldn't have been affected much. Score one for the lycan. *Not.*

"You know, Addie, you didn't have to wake up Dr. Wolfe. He even slept on the couch, probably afraid he couldn't hear me in the basement. Although we both know that's a load of crap as lycan hearing can pick up the most minute sound for miles."

"I didn't want to wake you. Besides, Forrest is an early riser. How are you feeling?"

"I'm much better, thanks. Dr. Wolfe is good at what he does, after all." Forrest couldn't help but laugh at the sheer irony of that statement. After all, he had not stayed exactly by her bedside. And had broken what should have been an immortal rule. Suddenly, he had lost all interest in the phone conversation. What had happened last night? He had had his share of girlfriends in his lifetime. But Gillian was different. Had last night's confession and kiss meant the same to her as it did to him? What would happen now? Would Gillian tell Addie about it? She shouldn't. He was an immortal; what was he doing? Throwing friendship and knowledge out the window, apparently. She hadn't said anything—at all. She had just walked away. He supposed he had always known Gillian tended to shy away from uncomfortable topics.

And he was pretty sure this one would qualify.

"Addie, I'm fine. I want to go to work. I'm sure Dr. Wolfe's life doesn't revolve around me; I'm sure he'd appreciate some time to himself while I go earn a paycheck."

"Tell *Dr. Wolfe* I wish him a good day."

"Addie—Damn it."

Forrest gulped as he heard Gillian swear. He was sure that their mutual black-haired vampire friend had just spoiled his morning. He heard Gillian take a deep breath, her hand brushing his as she handed him the phone back.

"Thanks," she said, giving him a thin smile as she sighed.

"You're welcome." He pulled the blanket away, revealing his sweatpants and his white undershirt. When at Gillian's place, he figured he would at least be decently semi-dressed. He was, after all, a guest at her house. When he was at his apartment, he really preferred just his boxers, as his lycan virus did make him conserve more body heat. He folded the blanket as he felt Gillian's eyes burning his back. He would tidy his mess, although he was sure Gillian wouldn't care one way or the other. Gillian wasn't the neatest person he knew.

"You hungry?" He heard her as he finished putting the blanket on the corner of the beige couch, next to the pillow that he had brought up from his cage downstairs.

"Dr. Wolfe, did you hear me?"

Forrest found himself face-to-face with Gillian, who was still massaging her wet hair. And in her bathrobe. And so his mouth opened and closed, with no words getting out.

Real smooth.

"Breakfast?" She raised her eyebrows. "You must be hungry since you didn't eat anything since who knows when—"

"How are you? How are you feeling?" Forrest asked. It must have been a little late for his regular breakfast time, as he could see sparks of sun shining through the thin openings of the richly colored purple and lilac curtains of Gillian's living room, but he wasn't hungry. He couldn't remember the last time that had happened.

Gillian cleared her throat, going back to massaging her hair. Forrest knew she hated when he answered a question with another one. But he couldn't help but worry about her, and about what her answer would tell him about the repercussions of last night.

"I'm fine," she replied. "A little sore. Geez, I've got to get out of here. I'm getting cabin fever. But otherwise, no complaints." She smiled. It was a different kind of smile, not one of politeness, but one that actually reached her eyes. But her answer further confused him. A scientist by heart, he had to put a quantity to what "fine" meant. Hadn't she just said that she felt claustrophobic and sore? Then how could she feel fine? "So, what do you want?" she continued, watching him.

"What?"

"Food, Dr. Wolfe. Meat? Eggs? Maybe both? Have you actually eaten while you've been here?"

"You don't cook, Gillian. In fact, in all the years I've known you, you've never used your stove for anything other than potion-brewing."

"I can cook. I just prefer not to. But since you've taken such good care of me lately, I figured—"

He couldn't help but laugh. "Such good care of you? Is that what people are calling it these days?" He should have been worried about offending her. But since she picked that morning to be perky, he supposed he could play that game as well. And she didn't look the least bit offended.

"You mean overall . . . or just last night?"

Her suggestive attitude brought the next obvious question to mind.

"How much medication did you take last night, Gillian?"

"Really? I feel fine."

"And I'm glad for that, Gillian, I am. You look much better. But after what happened last night, I need to apologize."

"Oh, I forgot, you need any laundry done? Since today is laundry day, I figured I'd offer."

"Gillian."

"And since you're up for babysitting today, too, sorry about that, I thought maybe we'd maybe could go out for lunch or something. I owe you a meal after all."

"Gillian, okay, maybe I should start by apologizing." Forrest passed his hand through his hair. His dreams about being with Gillian hadn't included this version of the moment, or even the morning after. "According to the prescription I gave you, you would have been heavily medicated, and I shouldn't have taken advantage of the situation."

Forrest's attempt at an apology was shut down as Gillian's lips pressed against his. Truth be told, he never thought he would feel such a perfect sensation again. And this time, he didn't hesitate to respond as his hand cupped the side of her face.

She pulled away. "Dr. Wolfe, has anyone ever told you that you talk too much?"

"Gillian, I—" Forrest sighed. Her closeness and fresh honeysuckle scent were almost too much.

"You could've just told me you wanted to postpone the food." Gillian leaned in for a kiss again.

She had made the first move twice already this morning. That had to mean something. But wasn't Addie coming this afternoon? One more touch of Gillian's lips against his and those thoughts flew to the back of his mind. He wasn't about to let logistics ruin this moment. Addie could wait until after the kisses were over.

Chapter 25

Click

*C*Gillian's eyes opened as she heard her house door unlock. She had always been a light sleeper, despite Addie's belief to the contrary. But last night, thanks to her hairy babysitter, hadn't been particularly restful. And, well, it's not like this morning had improved things. Had it?

She attempted to get out of bed. She was restless anyway. And where was Forrest? After a very light, uncomfortable breakfast this morning, filled with small talk about the weather and interesting hospital cases, neither of them willing to talk about the elephant in the room, he had offered to do her laundry and sent her off to rest. She hadn't protested—at least he was back to his old, cheery self. In fact, he seemed cheerier. Anyway, she had a lot of thinking to do, which she had planned to do while she was supposed to be *resting*. Well, she could multitask. And the first thought on her mind had been that kissing an immortal back had been a stupid thing to do. And taking the initiative to kiss him this morning had been . . .

Also a stupid thing to do.

That's as far as her mind had gotten.

But wasn't he the one that had to come up with those answers? After all, he had kissed her first, and as far as kissing immortals went, he had a lot more experience than her. The only romantic encounter she had had with an immortal had been four years ago. And she didn't want that experience repeated, which begged the question: *Why the hell did I kiss him, not once, but three times?* Not to mention there was a real possibility that Forrest had feelings for Addie. But he had kissed her first. That had to mean something. But he had let Addie bite him. No one did that willingly unless . . . Gillian let out a deep breath. She could already feel a headache starting. How typical.

"Damn it." She darted out of bed and closed herself in the bathroom. She smiled at her cat, who was sleeping on top of the laundry hamper. Addie must be downstairs. No one else had a key to her house. And Dagonet and Addie weren't on the friendliest of terms. Addie's temper rivaled the cat's in stubbornness and instant temper tantrums, so they did better apart. She sighed as she looked at her reflection in the mirror. Addie likely wouldn't come into her room or call her. She would assume she was asleep. But she *would* go in search of Forrest. If Gillian didn't beat him to it, would he say something? What was there to tell? Why had he kissed her, damn it?

"Stop," she told herself, putting her hair into a quick ponytail. She'd have to figure out something to tell Addie. In the meantime, she might as well go downstairs and get the afternoon started.

❖

"There she is! Good morning, Gill." Addie waved at her as she descended the stairs. "Or afternoon, I should say. It's past lunch. But the patient looks a lot better. Thank you, Forrest."

"My pleasure, Addie." He nodded to Addie before setting his eyes on Gillian. And she swore the glance lasted a little too long. "Gillian."

"Dr. Wolfe," she replied as nonchalantly as she could muster. She hoped it worked. Addie didn't appear to notice anything.

"Come sit down. I brought lunch." Addie stood up, making her way to the kitchen.

"So, how is the patient feeling?" Forrest glanced at Gillian as she took her seat at the dining room table—as if the jumping jacks in her heart weren't enough. Gillian found that she wasn't feeling like having lunch. Crawling under the bed until her mind either quieted or gave her some semblance of a solution sounded like a better idea.

"Stop that. You know I feel fine," she hissed. Suddenly, saying she felt uncomfortable was a huge understatement. She had no one to blame but herself, but she'd be lying if she said her lips weren't itching to feel his again.

"Yeah? No cabin fever to speak of?"

"Well, I can't help that. Did you find everything you needed for your shower?" She focused on his damp, dark-blond hair.

"Why, yes, thank you. Your coconut shampoo is a change though. One I could get used to." He shrugged, displaying a smug smile.

"Yes, well, you're going to have to go back to your apartment sooner or later."

"I suppose when you get back to work you won't need me around. But that doesn't mean I can't be around when you want me to be." Forrest reached for her hand, brushing his palm against hers.

"Forrest told me neither of you ate much, so I had Bee cook your favorites," Addie said as she came back carrying two plates. Gillian's hand went from Forrest's to her lap before the vampire could set the plate on the table. Thank goodness she had grown up with immortals and had learned a thing or two about reflexes. "Gillian isn't much of a cook, so I should've known today's breakfast wasn't much."

"Wow, thanks, Addie." Forrest lost no time digging into his rare meat and potatoes.

"I'll have you know I can make a decent meal, thank you," Gillian snapped.

"Oh, so you did cook?" Addie glanced at her.

"Well, no. It turned out that Dr. Wolfe wasn't hungry at the time."

"Forrest not hungry? That's a first." Addie raised her eyebrow while glancing at the werewolf.

"I was otherwise distracted." Forrest shrugged, winking Gillian in the process, which made her huff. Could he be any more obvious? He might as well come out and say it.

But say what? That he kissed a mortal? When was the last time that had happened? Was this a habit of his? Was this a meaningless experiment? What exactly could he gain by it? Would it happen again? Did she want it to?

"I'd say." Addie glanced at Gillian. "What's the matter, lost your appetite?" Gillian noticed the vampire's attention focused on her untouched egg salad sandwich.

"Yeah, I guess lack of a good night's sleep has caught up with me. But no worries, I'll save it for later." Gillian stood up. "Want some more, Addie?" She grabbed the red mug the vampire kept at her house.

The red color had been her idea. That way she didn't have to constantly see what Addie was drinking. She saw enough of it in the lab.

"No, I'm good, thanks. You can go back to sleep if you need to. I'll see Forrest out."

"Does this mean I'm clear for work tomorrow?"

"If the night is uneventful, yes. I'll be in the basement if you need me."

Gillian sighed. The unrelenting headache told her it was best to let Addie do what she wanted. Besides, at least she wouldn't have to deal with Forrest tonight.

"Fine. Thank you for everything, Dr. Wolfe." Gillian smiled thinly at him.

Forrest and Addie walked together to the door, but Gillian could hear their voices filtering into the kitchen.

"Is she not sleeping well?"

"Not lately."

"Oh, jeez. Is she having those nightmares again? "

"Oh, I wouldn't call it that."

"What would you call it then? Oh, for goodness sake, stop staring! She's probably already in her room. You need to do something, Forrest, if only for my own sanity. You're lucky she's so oblivious."

Chapter 26

Really? *It's the middle of the fucking night.*

Gillian groaned as she glanced at her clock. The blue lights flashed 2:00 A.M. back at her. The nausea was back. *One cup of tea should do it. I'll be right back, kitty.* Her cat didn't even stir, so it was safe to assume that he hadn't heard her.

Well, at least one of us is able to sleep soundly.

"Hey there."

Gillian gasped, but before she could drop her cup, she felt Forrest's hand steadying her own. The hairs on her arms stood up at his touch. Wasn't Addie supposed to be staying tonight? Well, it's not like sweatpants and a tank top were the sexiest things she owned. Regardless, she crossed her arms.

"Sorry, didn't mean to scare you."

Gillian reached for the kitchen light and turned on the kettle with a wave of her wrist. What was the point of keeping it off? Sleep was lost at this point. Her heart had resumed its werewolf-provoked jumping jacks.

"What are you doing here, Dr. Wolfe?" Her hand tried to tame her hair. *Nice try. And why would you care so much? Do you really think an immortal wants to be with you? Wake up!*

"Wanted to make sure you were taken care of." He shrugged, letting go of her hand. "What kind of tea did you want?"

"I thought Addie—"

The werewolf put his finger on her lips. "Wait for it," he whispered.

She took a deep breath as she willed her heart to calm down, her hand brushing his away from her face. There it was. Addie's snores could be heard from her basement coffin.

"Yep, she's been a little short of sleep lately." He finished up with one of his gorgeous smiles. She had to get back to the matter at hand. And the fact that Forrest hadn't caught up on his own lack of sleep.

"So have you. Shouldn't you be resting as well?" she pointed out.

"I'm fine, Gillian. I've lost all my sleep willingly." Forrest gave her another smile, his hand caressing the side of her face. She couldn't help but sink into his touch, her eyes closing.

"What do you want?"

Her eyes opened at the sound of his voice.

"What?"

"Did you want chamomile tea?"

"Oh, yes, thank you. You know, I'm fine. I can make the tea myself. You should get some rest."

"It's all right, Gillian, I slept earlier. Addie and I

took turns. Besides, you wouldn't be here if you were feeling fine."

"It's just a little nausea."

"I figured. Part of the pain med's secondary effects, I'm afraid."

"Yeah." She sighed as she reached for her water pitcher in the fridge.

"Do you want to sit down? I'll have this ready in a minute." He turned to the cup cabinet.

"No, thanks. I'll just take it upstairs. That way you can rest too. Feel free to use the couch if the basement is a little too loud for you." Gillian could still hear Addie's snores. Wow, she had to be really sleep-deprived if her snores were traveling through the coffin and through the closed basement door. "I can bring a blanket and a pillow for you."

"Gillian, I'm fine. In fact, I think I'll help myself to some tea as well." He reached for the teapot.

"Okay, then. Thanks for this." She took the mug he offered her, the chamomile scent reaching her nostrils. "Good night, Dr. Wolfe." She turned to the stairs and heard Forrest's whispered laugh.

"Gillian, seriously, what will it take for you to call me by my first name?"

Gillian's eyebrows furrowed. It was after two in the morning. He wanted to bring this up now?

"Dr. Wolfe, I don't—"

"There you go again. Is it that you like the lycan association? Because given what's happened during the last two days I'd say we're a little past the *friends by association* category."

"Dr. Wolfe." This time she couldn't figure out a quick way to squeak out of the conversation. "What happened between us—"

"And I've never heard you call Addie 'Dr. Brystol.'"

"Funny you should mention Addie."

"What's that?"

"I feel bad, given how close you two are, to have come between you like I did."

"Come between us? How? Oh . . . please tell me you're joking." Forrest's face went from puzzled to really stressed in a matter of seconds as he walked towards her.

"Well, I know Addie doesn't bite just anyone and you did offer to let her."

"Yes, because she was about to pass out!" He was yelling. He never yelled.

Gillian's eyes opened wide.

"Come on, Gillian, you didn't actually think I would—after we—you kissed—oh, good grief." Forrest made his way to the sink, his untouched tea poured down the drain.

Forrest had never been mad at her, ever. And he was still talking loudly. She had never witnessed him raising his voice, to anyone. The fact that he was doing it with her hurt, she had to admit. Especially since she was trying to get at the truth. If he had let Addie bite him, what did he want with her? What could she offer him? She was a mortal, and she sucked at magic, which was the one thing she was supposed to be good at.

"I'm sorry, Dr. Wolfe, I didn't mean—"

"Stop! Just . . . stop calling me that. It makes what happened between us sound—well, maybe that's what it was to you." His eyes bored suddenly into hers. "Is that the case? I mean, I know the first night you were on that medication and I shouldn't have, but—"

"Oh, for heaven's sake, drop it!" Gillian cleared her throat as she realized how loud her voice was now. "It's not like I didn't realize what the fuck I was doing."

"Well, that's exactly what you're making it sound like! But since you're bringing it up, do enlighten me. If you obviously knew what you were doing, why did you do it?"

"Well, I thought it was pretty obvious."

"Not quite, it seems."

"Let's try it your way, why don't we, Dr. Wolfe?"

"What the hell does that mean?"

"Why does a woman actually kiss a man?"

"I know why I would do it, kiss a woman that is, but since you brought Addie up . . ."

"Attraction is a little difficult to explain, isn't it, Dr. Wolfe? Well, maybe not to an immortal who has had probably lots of time to sort through unresolved baggage."

"Attraction? Is that what this is? Is that all it is?"

"Well, it's certainly part of it, isn't it? I mean, if I didn't find you physically attractive, I wouldn't have—"

"Yeah, that's nice, Gillian. We've known each other long enough. That might work for some high school idiot that doesn't know any better."

"It's been a day. What would you call it?"

"I'd call it more than that or you wouldn't have kissed me this morning. Or maybe you'd like to count it as one occasion, is that what you're telling me?"

"I'm just saying it's a little too soon."

"Oh, okay. So how am I supposed to react then? Are we back to your *friends by association* category?"

"All right, maybe you should tell me then what an immortal would want with a mortal."

"What I want?" He moved closer to her still, taking her by her shoulders. "I want you. And I'll let you in on a little secret: immortality has nothing to do with it," he whispered, brushing her lips with his shortly afterwards.

Gillian couldn't help but moan as his tongue played with her lower lip. She opened her mouth under his, her free arm going around his neck.

Addie's voice rose up from the basement stairs. "Jeez, Forrest, what is the ruckus about? Getting out of a coffin is no picnic, you know."

Gillian backed away from Forrest, managing to spill her tea on him in the process. "Ah! Oh, I'm so sorry!"

"Gillian, it's fine."

"Here, let me clean it up."

"Clean what up?" Addie burst around the corner. "Gillian, what are you still doing up? Is everything all right?"

Gillian turned to Addie. "No! I mean, I was feeling nauseous and Dr. Wolfe was kind enough to make me some chamomile tea that I just managed to spill down his shirt."

"Okay, we get you're a hazard at two in the morning," Addie replied. Gillian could swear there was a tinge of sarcasm in her voice.

"Well, we were just talking."

"Talking? Is that what that was? I wouldn't be surprised if you guys woke up the neighbors. Is there anything I should know about?"

"I'm sorry we woke you, Addie," Gillian apologized. "And actually, I should help Dr. Wolfe clean up."

"Oh, no worries, Gillian. *Dr. Wolfe* can clean himself up. I'll see you ladies tomorrow." Forrest waved goodbye, reaching for his gray jacket.

"Forrest, it's two in the morning." Gillian heard Addie intervene before she could. She had been thinking along the same lines, immortality notwithstanding.

"Fresh air will do me good." Gillian noticed he didn't even look at her.

"Well, if you insist on going to your apartment, let me at least give you a ride. It's chilly outside and the lights haven't turned on. You don't want to walk on a dark road."

"Nonsense, Addie. It's not far. Besides, the patient here needs to be taken care of." Forrest motioned to her as he spoke, Gillian noticed, but still did not look at her.

"The *patient here* is feeling fine, thanks. And I already told you it's perfectly all right to spend the night on the couch if you don't feel like going to the basement."

"That was before I got chamomile tea spilled all over me."

"Well, take your shirt off. I'll get you a new one."

"It's fine, Gillian, I have to do laundry anyway. Addie will take care of you. It's pretty obvious you're tired of having me around."

"Damn it, that's not what I said and you know it."

"Don't worry, Gillian. You've made your feelings quite clear. Good night."

Forrest didn't even bother smiling at her as he nodded to Addie, closing the door swiftly behind him.

"Okay, you want to tell me what the hell just happened?" said Addie. "Because I've never seen Forrest so mad. And yelling! He even left his jacket here, and it is cold tonight for a warm-blooded immortal. Did something happen between you?"

"I don't want to talk about it." Gillian waved as she made her way to the stairs, signaling an end to anything further coming out of Addie's mouth. "Make yourself at home if you want to stay and I'll see you tomorrow. Well, in a few hours, anyway."

"O . . . kay."

Gillian heard Addie's obvious puzzlement. But she wasn't in the mood to indulge the vampire. After all, it hadn't worked out so well with the werewolf. She supposed she had that much more to worry about tomorrow. She could feel the headache coming again already. It was barely two in the morning, and it had already been a long day.

Chapter 27

G illian sighed as she opened the door to her office, taking her baby-blue coat off. "Ugh," she said as she set sight on her desk. There they were. A vase of red roses staring back at her.

"Damn you," she whispered, putting her purse next to her desk chair.

These were undoubtedly new ones, as the original ones Forrest had brought her days ago had been collateral damage in the fight with Addie. That meant Forrest had been here this morning—and of course there was a card.

You will always be mine.

Now it was her turn to ask what the hell that meant. *No time like the present to find out*, she thought as she picked up the receiver.

"Dr. Brystol."

"Hey, Addie, it's Gillian. Is Dr. Wolfe with you?" If there was one thing she could always count on, it was the fact that her friends were always in close proximity to each other. She didn't want to admit it, but right now, that thought was causing a knot on her stomach.

"Forrest is in surgery, Gill. Why? Is there anything you need?"

"No, it's not important. I'm sure I'll see him later."

"We'll be down for lunch at about twelve thirty. Join us?"

Gillian knew what that meant. Meeting Addie with her green cup at the table, red cup was for home. If anyone asked, she was on a smoothie diet.

"Yeah, I'll be there."

"Okay. See you later."

Gillian put down the receiver and sighed. Fortunately, she could count on work to provide the perfect distraction between now and when she could tell Forrest Wolfe exactly what she thought of him. Now she just had to figure out what that was.

❖

Gillian sipped what was left of her hot tea with honey. Lunch had come and gone. And Dr. Wolfe's surgery had run late.

Not that she didn't appreciate some quality time with Addie, but she wanted to talk to Forrest when she was actually in the mood to deal with those issues.

She glanced at the vase of red roses once again, the cryptic note perched beside it. If it wasn't for last night's fight . . .

She laughed when she found herself heading down that line of thought. Their relationship had always bordered on excessive civility. She had always thought she was friends with him because he was friends with Addie. Not that a friendship with him didn't have its perks, one of them being that more times than not she had a lunch companion. Not to mention that she could always leave Addie's blood with him when she wasn't around and she could be sure Addie would get it, no questions asked. After all, being friends with immortals was a tough job, discretion being the key word everywhere they went. So it sometimes was nice to have someone to talk about it with.

She buried her face in her hands. This had been her fault, not his. She had pushed too far when she had kissed him not once, but twice. What had she been thinking, getting involved with an immortal? How old was he again? He had been an attending when she was fourteen. And who knew how long it had taken him to get there? Years? Decades? Centuries? Well, regardless, he was significantly older than her, even if he definitely didn't look it. And he had helped Addie practically raise her. That fact alone should have barred her from even thinking about kissing him again, no matter how appealing his lips were, and how great a kisser he was.

Okay, so why *had* she kissed him? What had she been trying to find? She already knew he was attractive, even if he was adorably unaware of it. But she knew better than to invest in a relationship with an immortal. She thought again about Forrest's cryptic note. For the life of her, she had never known Forrest to be the possessive type.

Well, she supposed there were a lot of things she didn't know about him.

"Gillian? You okay? Addie told me you were looking for me this morning."

Gillian straightened up in her chair. The source of her thoughts was right in front of her.

Chapter 28

"Good afternoon, Dr. Wolfe. So, this is what Addie meant when she insisted I hold on to your lunch." She dangled a container in front of him.

"Thanks. May I?" He motioned to the chair across from her.

"Sure. I'll assume you're not in a hurry to get back to the on-call room, then."

"I have my beeper if anyone needs to get a hold of me. Now, can you please stop beating around the bush and tell me what you need?"

"Why would you automatically assume I need anything?" She felt a bit insulted. It was the first time in a long time that Forrest didn't seem happy to see her, which wouldn't explain the vase in front of her. Maybe all he wanted to hear was an apology. She wasn't sure he deserved one.

"No offense, Gillian, but you've never called me in here unless that's the case. And after last night, I doubt you'd change that pattern now."

Gillian sighed. She didn't want to get into another argument. Merely the prospect of it threatened to give her yet another migraine. After a couple of days of those, suffice it to say she'd had enough. "I see you're not interested in friendly chatter. I'll get right to the point then. To tell you the truth, I'm not sure you deserve it, so I'll just put that out there first."

"What?" Forrest raised an eyebrow.

"Well, that's what you're looking for, isn't it? An apology? That's why you were here so early."

"Early? I had trouble sleeping, therefore was late to work this morning, missed lunch, I'm starving, and I have another surgery in an hour. What are you talking about?"

"Fine. So, you're not going to admit messing around on my desk then." She rarely got truly angry with him. Yes, she was irritated by his excessive politeness, and his habit of doing Addie's bidding had frustrated the hell out of her. But before their attraction had gotten the better of them, they never argued. But everything had exceptions. So much for not having an argument now.

"Messing around on your desk? Why would I do that? Especially when you're not here? Why, is anything missing, Gillian?"

"No, Dr. Wolfe, more like something added." She pointed at the vase. "The roses? Noticed those?"

"Oh. Oh! I see. I'm sorry, Gillian."

Gillian smiled thinly as Forrest fidgeted in his seat. Finally! Why the hell had that taken so long? Couldn't he at least be direct about it? No matter how irritated he was at her, she figured she deserved that much.

"I'll replace the vase Addie broke. Jeez, I was so worried about you I completely forgot. But if those are going to remind you of that, I'll just stick with something other than flowers."

"No, Dr. Wolfe, that's not it."

"So you don't want it replaced? I completely understand."

"No, damn it. So you didn't put these here?"

"What? Oh, no. If I were going to give you something, I'd give it to you in person. I know you don't like surprises. Why, you don't know who—"

"Never mind. I'm sure I'll find out soon enough."

"I can ask Addie. I'm sure she would know."

"No. It's fine. I . . ." Gillian glanced at the note again. Suddenly, she felt her heart violently thumping against her chest.

There was only one person who had called her "his." And if Forrest wasn't responsible . . .

"Gillian, are you all right? You look nauseated."

Before she realized what was going on, Forrest was by her side, his hand on her face.

"I'll go get Addie. Are you dizzy? Maybe I should go get orange juice."

"I'm fine!"

"You don't look fine. You could still have pain medication in your system. I can go get some food if that is what you prefer, but sugar is best for something like this, per your mother."

"No, no, could you—just stay for a minute?" She pressed his hand farther against her face. Strangely, the warmth radiating from his touch ameliorated the clamminess she was feeling. She sighed, her eyes closing.

She heard Forrest sigh as well, his other hand on her arm, pulling her to him. She fell effortlessly into his embrace.

"Gillian, talk to me. What's going on?" he whispered.

"I'm sorry," she whispered back, breathing in his musky scent. "I shouldn't have done this. You're an immortal. I knew that. You deserve better."

"We don't have to talk about this now." Forrest hands went up and down her lower back, producing a soothing sensation that also gave her goose bumps.

"I don't want you to get hurt. You shouldn't want to be with me, if you knew what I did."

"Hey." He pulled her away from him, his hands back on her face. She found herself looking into those gorgeous gray eyes. "I'm not going anywhere."

Before she knew it, he was kissing her softly.

"Forrest, we have surgery in thirty. You done? I thought we would go quickly over the case. Oh, excuse me."

Gillian sighed, pulling away to see a very smug Addie smirking in the doorway.

Chapter 29

"Never mind. I'll just see you in the OR," Addie finished, and Gillian saw her broad smile.

Well, she seems to have no problem with this, whatever this is.

"No, he should go with you. Wouldn't want him to be late." Gillian smiled thinly at Addie, then glanced at Forrest.

"Yeah, I should go scrub in." Forrest stood up, unable to look at her eyes, his cheeks a hot crimson color, no doubt matching her own. At least she wasn't the only one uncomfortable with the situation at hand.

"Fine. But I promise to return him to you soon." Addie couldn't hide her fangs from her smile this time. This time though, Gillian found the gesture adorable, not frightening. Her friend was a vampire, the other one was a werewolf. That was just part of who they were. And that would have to be all right. If her mother had trusted them, why shouldn't she?

Gillian nodded, still smiling. There was no way to deny it now. She found that she didn't want to. If Addie was indeed okay with this, them, she was also the perfect person to turn to for advice. She suddenly felt like a weight had been lifted off her shoulders. Maybe today would turn out to be a good day after all.

"I'll see you later, Gillian." Gillian closed her eyes as Forrest kissed her forehead.

"Yeah." She caressed his hand as he let go.

Addie paused at the door. "Ooh, roses."

Gillian's eyes went to the vase.

"Nice touch, Forrest." Addie gave the werewolf a thumbs up.

Shit.

"I didn't give them to her."

"I'll see you guys later!" Gillian waved at them, hoping to shut Forrest up. She would take care of the matter before Addie heard of it; she'd make sure of that. She should have taken care of the matter, a long time ago. She had waited far too long. Four whole years.

Gillian stood up once her friends turned the corner, briskly making her way to the bathroom. She tried hard not to cry as she threw up the contents of that afternoon's lunch.

Chapter 30

"So, how long has this been going on?" Addie glanced at Forrest as she positioned the scalpel.

"What's that?" Forrest looked at her from his chart.

"Seriously, Forrest. I walk in on the two of you and you won't even extend me that courtesy? I mean, I know you're jumping up and down and all. I can practically see the smug smile through your mask."

Forrest shrugged, and Addie could see he was blushing too.

"It's just been a few days, Addie. We haven't even talked about it. I mean, it's not like I haven't tried, but Gillian—"

"I know Gillian can be difficult, Forr."

"She's hung up on the, you know, lifetime issue."

"Ah, yes, I see."

"I can't blame her, her mother and all, but does she honestly think I would hurt her?"

"I don't think her mother is the issue here, Forrest. It's her ex."

"Pardon?"

"Okay, I see you haven't gotten to that yet. I think she should be the one to give you the details. But her last real relationship—well, let's just say it didn't end the way she envisioned."

"Are you talking about the guy she was dating when we met?"

"Yep, one and only."

"But he treated her like crap."

"Well, she did leave him. But it was shortly after she found out Bridget was really sick—I mean, not getting better. So it was like it all came crashing down at the same time for her. Know what I mean?"

"Absolutely. But wait, what does that have to do with me? He wasn't like me, was he? You were the first she got to hang out with, right? Why does she keep bringing the I-word up?"

"Because he was more like you than you think . . . or should I say, like me," Addie whispered.

❖

2009

"You're sure this will work?" Sean asked, and Gillian could tell he was hesitating. She couldn't blame him. But this was the only way of ensuring that their love would indeed last forever. No one would be able to separate them. And she would finally be able to get her mother off her back about her boyfriend.

"Yeah. It will hurt for like a second. But it'll be worth it."

"And this guy is legit?"

"Yeah, he was in the army with a friend of my mom's."

"You talking about that hot black-haired chick? Why couldn't she do it? This would've been a lot more pleasant, I got to tell you."

"You want this to get back to my mom? She'd never approve. Besides, you want to be with me forever, don't you?"

"Hell yeah, you're really hot, babe."

"Then trust me on this one, Sean."

"All right, you guys made it." The vampire was suddenly right in front of them. "Ready to live forever?" he asked, as Gillian's cell phone rang.

❖

2013

"Gillian, hey."

Gillian's eyes opened at the sound of Forrest's soothing voice.

"What are you still doing here, huh?" Forrest's hand settled on her cheek, stroking it softly.

"I was waiting for you," Gillian said, clearing her throat as she realized her voice sounded raspy. She couldn't be glamorous when she woke up, no matter how hard she tried or even what time of day the waking up took place.

"You didn't have to do that, Gill. Want me to drive you home?"

"We need to talk, Forrest. And this time I'm asking," Gillian sighed, attempting to get up from her couch. "I didn't want to miss you."

"So you left a message with Kathy. She told me to come straight here," he said, referring to the head nurse that day. "It's late, Gillian, let's get you home. Have you had dinner yet?"

"Forrest, I don't have time to mess around. I have to tell you this. You deserve to know."

"Okay. What is it?"

"Not here. Can you step out for a while?"

"Yeah. Let me get the Volvo."

"Don't bother. I'll take you." Gillian took hold of Forrest's scrub top, pulling him to her.

"Gillian, what are you . . . " Forrest laughed as Gillian decreased the distance between them.

"I'm not going to kiss you. You'll be glad I didn't."

Chapter 31

"Okay, I'm sorry. I should've given you a little warning. I should've known. Addie reacts exactly the same way. Can I get you anything? You'll be starving in a minute. I've got bacon in the fridge."

"Are you out of your mind?" Gillian heard Forrest's voice just before the sound of vomiting.

Gillian sighed. At this pace, she would never tell him what she desperately wanted him to know. She supposed she could—no, talking about how she created a vampire didn't sound like a topic she could do while Forrest was vomiting. She couldn't stop walking back and forth in her violet-decorated bedroom. Focusing on the cinnamon candle or the crocheted bears didn't help either. She had to tell him, before both of them got so excited at the possibility of being together that they forgot how many things were stacked against them—immortality being the fore-most in Gillian's mind.

The bathroom door opened. She smiled thinly, hoping she looked apologetic. To say that Forrest had looked better was an understatement. His blond hair was matted and wet, no doubt from sweat and water from the faucet, his scrubs looked wrinkled, like they had come out of an overstuffed drawer, and he actually looked pale. Gillian was shocked that he was capable of looking this way, especially with the quantity of medium-rare meat that he consumed daily.

"Oh, Forrest, gosh, I'm sorry!"

"Ah, there you go again."

"What?" Gillian raised her eyebrows as he actually smiled. And even though he looked like hell, she still found the smile adorable.

"You called me by my first name. You've done it at least three times today. If this is what it takes for you to warm up to me, feel free to zoom me whenever you want." He winked at her.

"Nah, I think you've had enough zooming to last awhile. Can I get you anything? Do you want to sit down?"

"I'll be fine, Gillian. Now, what was it you couldn't wait to talk to me about?"

"Okay, but I'll feel better if you lie down."

Forrest climbed onto Gillian's quilted bed.

"Thanks."

"For you, anything."

"Not so sure you'll feel that way after I finish," Gillian whispered, though it was more to herself than to him.

"What's that?"

"Ever been curious why I don't want to be immortal?"

"I thought the fact that your mother—I'm sorry, can I—"

"It's okay, Forrest. You're right. But my mind was set before she passed away. Her death did stop me. But not before I did something stupid."

"What?"

"Forrest, you're not the first immortal I've been with."

❖

"Gill, you here?" Addie came through the crystal doors of Gillian's office. Lights out was a sure sign that Gillian had already bid good riddance to the workday. Addie couldn't blame her. Gillian had to be exhausted. But then again, so was she. Back-to-back surgeries after lunch had her starving. She hoped Gillian had left some blood for her, though she supposed she could go to Gillian's house in search of her nourishment if there was none left here. But she definitely didn't want to disturb her while she was sleeping. Or maybe she was spending some time with Forrest. Just the thought of it brought a smile to her lips despite her stomach's angry growling and her growing weakness. That was the dark side about being undead—there was no extra nourishment that the body could use if you accidentally missed your feeding time. Very much like a diabetic, she needed to keep her food times straight. Unfortunately, such a task proved to be a tad difficult when one was a surgeon.

Still smiling, she took a green travel mug from the fridge, her eyes fixated on the red roses on top of Gillian's desk. *Such a nice touch, Forrest. So thoughtful after a fight. And Gillian loves red roses.*

Her eyes opened wide as she glanced at the note perched against the flower base. *You will always be mine.*

"Oh, shit." Addie put the mug down and picked up the note.

She knew Forrest well enough to know that he had never been possessive. There was only one man who had ever called Gillian his. The last man, and frankly the only man, that Gillian had ever been serious with.

Addie scoffed. At the age of seventeen, he could hardly be called a man. But now he would be about twenty-one, and not only that, he was immortal, by Gillian's own doing. And here he was again, seemingly intent on having Gillian in his life. But how had he found her? Never mind why Gillian had kept the bouquet in the first place. There was no question: Gillian had let it slip and told someone she shouldn't have, he had kept tabs on her somehow, or he had formed a connection and kept it through . . . *He couldn't have. She wouldn't have let him, not until . . . Oh fuck. She'd better not have.* Addie didn't know whether to feel mad, frustrated, or downright scared. Gillian's mother had entrusted her with Gillian, her most prized possession. How was she supposed to protect her if she didn't know what she had done four years ago with her stupid boyfriend?

Addie dropped the roses, complete with the vase, into the trash can and took the card with her. She didn't even flinch when she heard the crystal shattering. Just as she was about to turn off the lights in the office and go give Gillian a piece of her mind, the door opened.

"Hi, Addie. Did I miss Gillian?"

"Oh, it's you. Yes, Josh, you did. But there's some blood in the fridge if you're hungry." She took a drink from her mug.

"Oh, sweet, thanks. Boy, that surgery was a killer. I think my back will hurt in the morning no matter where I sleep tonight."

"Not in the mood for small talk, Josh. Could you please take the blood and go?"

"Yeah, I see that. What was wrong with the flowers?"

"Wrong sender," she said.

"Oh, what's going on? Trouble in paradise? I wondered how long her lycan infatuation would last."

"This isn't about Forrest, Josh! Although I suppose it will be now."

"You lost me."

"They're from Sean. Forrest would have never written something like this." She gave him the note.

"Sean? How does he know she's here? . . .

"He's back. And Gillian is going to tell me why."

Chapter 32

"O ... kay." Forrest shifted against Gillian's pillow. "I mean, technically you are because you were born immortal and this guy wasn't but—"

"So you fell for a vampire?" Forrest's eyebrows furrowed.

"Well I ... technically, he wasn't."

"That explains your reluctance to be with me."

"I don't want to hurt you."

"Gillian, I can see this is difficult for you. But I still want to be with you if you'll have me. Your past matters little to me."

"It does?"

"We've all made mistakes. The truth is, I care a lot about you, Gillian. And I would like to actually date you, if you'll have me." Forrest glanced at her, grazing his palm on her cheek.

"What?" *Way to go! Now he's going to think I don't want to! Wait, do I?*

"I realize this might scare you a little, and please, it's okay if you don't want to."

"That's really sweet, but I don't think I deserve it."

"Tell you what, let's just take it slow. One date, nothing formal. What do you say I take you out tomorrow? Anywhere you want. We'll have a nice quiet dinner, and I can answer all your questions."

Gillian's lips effectively stopped Forrest midsentence.

"Is that a yes?" Forrest chuckled when they parted for air. But Gillian just leaned in once more.

❖

Gillian hastily combed her hair with her fingers. She could see her reflection on the elevator's silvery door while it took her down, her office being her final destination. She couldn't help but look at her watch once again. Their serious talk had lasted longer than both of them had anticipated. Well, the reason being that there had been more than just talk; she hoped she had spritzed enough perfume on her to cover up Forrest's scent. So much for taking it slow. What was wrong with her lately? It was like with Forrest she had no control over herself when it came to wanting to touch him at every place imaginable. This afternoon she had gotten her wish, and it had been… She hadn't lost control with someone since . . .

Gillian sighed. It had been a reluctant conversation, but they had talked about it. So perhaps now, finally, she could put Sean behind her once and for all. The thought of it made her breathe out in relief. Now, if she could just finish her last administrative duties and make sure the black fridge was stocked. And those flowers . . . yep, she knew just what to do with them.

Gillian's brows furrowed as the elevator door opened. A glance toward the end of the hallway told her someone was in her office.

The janitor usually gets in at ten. Gillian glanced at her watch. Linda, the custodian, had at least an hour before her shift began. *Forrest is probably hungry.* She shrugged. *I told him to eat before coming back. Well, I hope he gets caught up with charts like he wanted.* Regardless, she couldn't blame him if he chose not to eat right before zooming him to the on-call room. He had made sure to request to Kathy that no one be present. He needed his rest. That was his excuse, anyway. He probably didn't want to scare anyone.

Gillian took out her badge automatically, the door to her office just a couple of seconds away.

"Gillian Anne, long time no see."

Gillian gasped as she set eyes on the one who would always remind her of her most foolish mistake.

Chapter 33

"Surprised to see me? I bet. Although you don't write, you don't call back. I did call you to no avail a couple of days ago. You still have the same phone number? Well, I didn't get an answer!"

"Eric? That was you?"

"Yes! And nothing! How else am I supposed to know how you are? One gets worried these days, you know, especially with all the dangerous things going on out there."

"And I suppose you've had nothing to do with that whatsoever, Eric."

"That hurts my feelings."

Gillian crossed her arms, suddenly feeling a chill that she couldn't remember ever feeling before.

Eric's eyes bore into hers. "You're afraid? I would've thought you'd be a full-fledged witch by now, able to take me on. Except . . . oh yes, there's immortality to account for."

"Come closer, I dare you," Gillian whispered.

"Foolish request, isn't it? Sean always said you were a spitfire."

"Yeah, I'm sure my ex has a lot of positive reviews about me."

"Ex? Oh, but he never told me you broke up. In fact, I believe he's under the impression you're still his. With the connection and all. Although I am sure he was puzzled, as was I, quite frankly, to discover you were bedding a lycan. I don't know, but it sounds like you two should communicate better. Goodness, are you all right? You look like you saw a ghost."

"Gillian, you forgot your jacket." Forrest came in and almost tripped over her, putting his arm around her waist to keep her from going forward.

"Oops, sorry about that," he said. "I thought you'd be alone."

"Well, well, if it isn't the lycan himself. You never struck me as a person who'd go for blonds, Gillian Anne."

"Oh, I'm sorry, I didn't know you had company. I can come back." Forrest backed away.

"Yes, please do, Forrest." Gillian pleaded.

"Oh, nonsense. We mustn't be rude to guests, after all. Shame, shame. I thought you'd be a better hostess." Eric pointed his index finger accusingly at Gillian before turning to Forrest. "Hello, Dr. Wolfe, I don't believe we've met. I'm Eric Callahan." He extended his hand.

"Pleasure." Forrest extended his hand before Gillian could block his access.

"Oh, cut the crap, Eric. You're not welcome here, so see yourself out."

"Ouch, Gillian Anne. We don't see each other in four years, and this is what I get?"

"Stop calling me that, damn it!"

"But that's your given name. What would Sean say about it?"

"What Sean thinks is no longer my business. Now get out."

"See, that's where you're wrong. After all, you're still connected. I'm sorry, Dr. Wolfe, did you know about this?"

"Leave Forrest out of this."

"Yes, leaving people out of things. She's good at that, isn't she?" Eric glanced at Forrest.

"Eric—" Gillian tried to interrupt.

"If I were her boyfriend, though, I'd want to know. I mean, wouldn't you, Dr. Wolfe? "

"Gillian, what's going on?" Forrest asked.

"Yes, *Gillian*, aren't you going to tell him what's been going on? I mean, it's only fair."

"Eric, stop it. There's nothing going on. It hasn't *gone on* for a long time."

"See, that's where Sean would disagree. You guys had something—hell, still have something, if he has anything to say about it."

"He does not."

"Lucky for you, I'm here and I can help fill in the blanks for the lycan." Eric's glance went from Gillian to Forrest.

"Excuse me, Mr. Callahan, is it? Sean Kennard being my girlfriend's ex is none of my business. Now, since Gillian asked you to leave, kindly do."

"Oh my! You even have the wolf trained, Gillian. I'm impressed. Not that a dog is hard to train. But I bet he doesn't know that you and Sean still share a blood connection, does he?"

Gillian breathed out, willing her rapidly beating heart to calm down before she reluctantly glanced at Eric. One look into his dark-brown eyes told her one thing—he was not bluffing.

"It's not true. That can't be possible. It's been—"

"Four years? True. But a skilled vampire can hold onto a connection for as long as he desires. Or, in the case of Sean, as long as it takes to find his beloved. I should know. I turned him—at your request, of course. Would've turned you if you hadn't had a sudden attack of conscience. Or was it fear of a little pain? It does hurt like a bitch, but it's worth it, if I do say so myself. Either way, you chickened out. And did I ever hear a thank you? I think not. But, I don't know, maybe you need another immortal to confirm it for you. Dr. Wolfe would know, having turned a vampire himself at another's request and all. What do you think?"

Gillian glanced at Forrest. His face grim, he nodded. He had turned Addie into a vampire. And had taken care of her during the aftermath. He would definitely know.

"There we go. I knew I was right!" Eric looked like a smug student receiving a perfect score on a pop quiz. "So, here's what it means for you, my dear little lady. Well, it's what I suggest anyway. Contact Sean before he's left with no choice but to do it himself. After all, you don't want to face a vampire in a bad mood, do you? I dare say you've experienced the most unpleasant consequences of such an event. Now, I think I've overstayed my welcome. I'll see myself out."

Gillian sighed, passing her hand through her face. Taking a deep breath, she glanced at Forrest. "Forrest, I—"

"Is it true?"

"You have to understand, I didn't know."

"Gillian, for once, answer the question I asked you." Forrest sounded forcefully restrained.

Gillian bit her lip. There was no way to sugarcoat this, just as there was no way that he would understand. "I was young, I had no idea. I just thought—"

"You just thought that if you were going to be a vampire, there was no way you'd spend eternity alone. So you had to assure yourself your boyfriend would stay with you and thought it would be a good idea to try out this *experiment* of sorts with him first?" Forrest sounded genuinely angry with her.

"Please don't say it like that. It sounds—"

"Offensive? Depraved? Heartless? Maybe even selfish? Because that's exactly what it was."

"I know, Forrest! I know! Just . . ."

"Just what? Let it go? How can I? He won't let you go. And after everything that happened, I can't say I blame him."

"How can you say that?" Gillian couldn't stop the tears in her eyes from clouding her vision. So much for being the strong witch she wanted to believe she had become.

"You're what? You're sorry? Wish everything would just go away? See, I thought that years of living with immortals would have taught you something. Obviously, I was mistaken. But let me give you your first lesson, since I'm here and I'm, well, an immortal. Immortality isn't something you can simply *let go* of. Unlike love, it seems."

"I know, believe me."

"But it turns out that's exactly what I'm going to have to do. It's very clear that you mean more to me than I matter to you."

"What? No, that's not true!" He looked so . . . detached. She wiped the tears off her face.

"In fact, I wonder, what am I to you? Was I just someone momentarily desirable to pass your time with? Or did you feel you needed another immortal to make you feel like you did when you were sixteen? Perhaps you grew tired of the idea of becoming a vampire and decided becoming a lycan was better? When were you going to tell me that?"

"Forrest, what I feel for you is—"

"What, real? It was certainly convenient. Damn it, Gillian!"

"Forrest, I do care for you."

"Yes, I suppose you do. After all, you do tend to, temporarily anyway, care for people who can get you out of your messes. Well, let me tell you something. I won't fix this for you. So if that's what you want, better lust after some other willing slave." Forrest turned on his heel toward the door.

"Forrest, please, stay," Gillian begged in what came out to be a horribly nasal voice. She needed to say what she felt. That at least was genuine, for the first time in a long time. But when Forrest turned around, she did not see compassion, but contempt.

"Does Addie know about this, Gillian?" His question was certainly unexpected, and another blow to her already fragile composure. "I didn't think so," he said. "After all, you wouldn't want to risk another vampire temper tantrum. Well, here's some more advice, and after this, I won't bother you again: tell her, or I will." He left.

Gillian slumped on her desk chair, hushing her cries as much as she could. Her nightmare had become a reality. And this time, not even magic could fix it.

Chapter 34

Gillian didn't know how long it was before she mustered the strength to zoom home. But before she knew it, her alarm clock was shouting angrily at her and it took all her willpower not to tell it exactly what she was thinking. After all, magic when she was angry spelled a recipe for disaster. The last time that happened she had had to call the window repairman. And having to explain how on earth the windows had exploded from the inside had been worse than sitting down at eight in the morning to take her med tech licensing exam. And this time, the day's rain made it chillier and drearier than usual.

She moaned sleepily as she made her way towards a morning shower. It didn't refresh her or make her feel any better.

"You thought I wouldn't find out, didn't you?"

Gillian gasped as she spotted Addie by her purple curtains just as she came out of the bathroom. She supposed she could feign ignorance and ask Addie what she was talking about, not to mention what she was doing at her house at six thirty in the morning. Being a night creature by both habit and nature, Addie was a notoriously bad morning person.

Gillian closed her eyes, willing her ever fast-beating heart to calm down. She should have expected this. Forrest had warned her. Even so, she was angry with him. Sure, he was angry himself and she really couldn't blame him, but couldn't he give her at least a day to deal with her own problems before being a tattletale?

"Addie, I don't know what Forrest told you, but—"

"Forrest has nothing to do with this, Gillian. I can't even believe you would bring him into this."

"I don't understand. Forrest didn't talk to you?"

"I found the note from the flowers. You thought you could hide it from me? To think I actually praised Forrest for the gesture."

"I was going to tell you."

"Really? When? When Sean made his way to your house and tried to make you a bit more like him? By the way, how does he even know where you work? Either he has some impressive detective skills for a vampire or—"

"Addie, please."

"Those nightmares, they weren't dreams at all, were they? He was trying to contact you, wasn't he?"

"Addie, I didn't—"

"Really now? Are you going to tell me you didn't let him bite you? That you had no idea how he found you? Do me a favor, Gillian, it's way past time you stopped lying to me."

"Addie, please."

"You're not immortal, Gillian! Damn it, when are you going to accept that your mother, for better or for worse, knew what she was doing when she appointed me your guardian? I don't know, maybe you lied to her too."

"Addie, I don't think my mother was wrong."

"And now I get to deal with this mess," Addie sighed. "I better talk to Forrest about it. Is that why you slept with him, Gillian? Don't you dare lie. So he would fix your mess?"

"No! Addie, I care for him. I would never."

"There's nothing that man wouldn't do for you. How can you throw that away?"

"No, I wouldn't!"

"Not. Another. Word. I swear if I hear so much as a peep out of you . . . " Addie sighed once again, passing her tongue through her now noticeably pointed incisors.

Gillian looked into Addie's misty green eyes. Closing her own brown ones, she prayed Addie would fight the transformation long enough that it wouldn't take place. This time, Forrest wasn't there to protect her. Still, the way she was feeling right now, she almost welcomed the idea of Addie ripping her throat out.

"You better stay out of sight, Gillian. We'll find a way to deal with your mess."

"Addie, you don't have to."

"I'm not doing it for you, Gillian. Your mother deserves more. I'm so glad she can't see what you've become."

"Addie, please!" Gillian couldn't stop the tears from prickling her skin as they rolled down her cheeks again. What she would not give to hug her mother right now. No matter what, her mother would know how to take care of this.

"Shush!" Addie said. She cleared her throat as Gillian bit her lip, tears still streaming down her face. "I'll see myself out." Gillian assumed she was leaving to fight her transformation, but she couldn't help but jump as she heard the front door slam shut.

Chapter 35

The ride on the elevator was eternal when Gillian finally made herself go to work. She had brought her car. She didn't trust herself to zoom while she was feeling so wretched. Although a few fractured bones sounded tempting. Anesthesia meant not having to think. However, that kind of hospital visit meant an angrier Addie. And having seen how Addie had barely controlled her vampire rage this morning—that was a risk she most definitely wasn't going to take. After all, she had Dagonet to think about.

She chuckled as she thought about her gray and white cat. As the last living remnant of her mother's life, Gillian would protect that feline until she stopped breathing.

"Oh, good, you're here. Emergency surgery has been scheduled and we need blood." Kristy, one of

Gillian's fellow med techs, greeted her as soon as she entered the lab. No chance to go to her office, but that was just as well. She needed the distraction.

"All right, where's the order?" Gillian searched for the paperwork on the computer.

"The surgery was last minute; the doctor didn't have time to put it in. They phoned me to do it. Just get me some O-neg and I'll deliver."

"Okay, who's the doctor?" Gillian asked as she glanced at the chart with blood orders for the day. She hated when something like this happened, as she preferred to be precise and thorough. But she knew that emergencies called for some rule bending, especially when the life of a patient was at stake.

"Dr. Brystol."

Gillian's hands immediately backed away from the counter, the chart forgotten.

"Pardon me?" Although she was all too familiar with emergencies, she was more familiar with vampire strengths. And Addie's many strengths included a speed like no other. No matter what, Addie always found a way to get the order in. She always said she was too old and too tired to deal with the paperwork and red tape that came after emergencies were taken care of, so she prided herself at being extra efficient in the moment.

Gillian didn't know exactly what was going on in the OR, but she did know one thing: these were not Addie's orders.

"It's her and the lycan in surgery. Just give me the O-neg and I'll deliver."

"What?" Gillian gasped as her eyes focused on the med tech's eyes. No tech, or anyone in their right mind, would call Forrest by any other name than

"Dr. Wolfe" at work. If anything, the hospital's few employees that knew of the doctor's true immortal nature had promised to be discreet. And there was no way a med tech, a worker low on the totem pole by hospital standards, would know of Forrest's love for rare red meat and fear of the full moon.

"Don't worry about it, Kristy, I'll deliver it. Take it easy for a few minutes, all right?" Gillian stayed long enough to see the med tech shrug. But those misty brown eyes didn't seem particularly human. Unless a vampire was channeling through . . . someone had spent the night with her ex, it seemed.

Gillian opened the door of the OR. This was very much not allowed, considering she was neither scrubbed in nor authorized to be there. And she was sure at least one person in that OR other than her was neither sterilized nor an authorized presence.

"Look out!" she cried.

The first surprised face she saw was Forrest's. Forrest, she noticed, was still preparing for the anesthesia delivery.

"Gillian! What . . . you're not sterilized! Get out!"

"Stop, it's a trap!" She looked at Addie, who was looking at her tools next to the gurney. Where was the surgical tech? Gillian found herself gasping desperately for breaths. She could feel the stress and confusion setting in. *What to do?* She frantically looked around. After Eric's visit last night, she had no doubt it was her that Sean was after. But of *course* he would go after her friends. Gillian had never been afraid of death, not since her mother had been taken so early and so suddenly. If anything, she longed to see her again, even if it was in the afterlife. But her friends, the ones that her mother had left her in charge of as well as in charge of her—she couldn't bear it if anything happened to them. But how could she defend them?

Gillian briefly felt the pints in her hands. She didn't even know why she had taken them. The blood order had been a sham. But if there was something vampires craved, it was in her hands, staring at her.

And the gurney wasn't moving.

"Addie, duck!" Gillian screamed as she threw the bags at the gurney. It didn't matter if she didn't have the greatest aim in the world. This had to work.

The blanket covering the patient on the gurney suddenly went to the floor and she found herself looking into brown eyes she thought she had long forgotten.

"Sean."

"Well, well, my love, long time no see."

Chapter 36

"Addie, look out!"

Sean stuck a scalpel in Addie's back. Gillian wasn't sure if she heard her own scream or Addie's.

Addie gasped and grabbed the gurney to stay on her feet.

"Addie!" Gillian ran to help support her. Just because Addie wasn't living in the standard manner—that is, with blood circulating through her veins and a beating heart—that did not mean she could not feel pain. *Right? Was that the case?* She couldn't remember asking Addie. She knew Forrest could feel pain, but he was a different species altogether.

Gillian, her vision clouded from the unshed tears pooling in her eyes, realized that four years of guardianship and a couple more years as friends was not nearly enough to get to know someone you loved.

Sixteen years had not been enough to get to know her own mother.

"I don't want to lose you too," she whispered.

Addie whirled out of Gillian's hold and tried to take Sean by his neck.

Gillian found her own feet seemingly stuck to the ground. *What the—I can't move!*

"And let you miss all the fun? I think not." Sean snickered.

Crack! Gillian heard Sean break Addie's arm. She landed on the floor next to where Forrest was transforming into a lycan.

"No!" Gillian yelled as she attempted to move. All she managed to do was slip and fall to the floor, her knee pulsating in pain.

Forrest launched himself at Sean. This was not what she had in mind when she had toned down Forrest's lycan rage. If he had his full lycan strength right now, this would be a fairer match. She sobbed, her tears now freely streaming down her cheeks as she tried in vain to crawl to Addie, who had lost consciousness. There was a steady stream of blood drizzling from her side.

She's immortal. She cannot die like this. Forrest howled as Sean threw him into the opposite wall, directly across from her.

Gillian's eyes desperately went from a very pale Addie to a gasping Forrest. She suddenly found her legs working. Her hands hastily cleared her tears as she crawled towards Forrest.

"Forrest, look at me, please," she whispered as she got closer to him. Her brows furrowed as she found him still gasping. When he and Addie had fought in her office he had gotten up faster than this. She saw a trail of blood coming from his gray fur. Her hands fumbled through his fur as she tried to find the source of the bleeding while he went back to human form.

His gray eyes looked at hers. He wasn't moving. His eyes looked glassy. She saw a shiny spot on his neck, now clouded by a trickle of red.

"It's no use. You can't," Forrest whispered.

"What? No!" Gillian could not help but sob as her hands touched what she could clearly discern to be the handle of a knife.

"Oh, please, no." She took off her sweater, cleaning around Forrest's neck only to discover the very thing she feared.

"Silver," she whispered, her sobs flowing freely now.

"Gillian, you can't fix it. Please, let go," Forrest said.

"No! Just . . . stay with me," Gillian whispered. But his gasping was subsiding now, and her was hand becoming crimson by the blood emanating from his neck.

"I can't lose you," she whispered once more.

She gasped when Forrest's trembling hand came to rest on her cheek. She could see what an effort he was making just to raise his arm.

"I love you," Forrest whispered, gasping between breaths.

"No . . . no!" Gillian caught his limp hand. His eyes seemed to focus on the ceiling, his rasping breaths diminishing.

Gillian glanced at Addie, who was pale and still unconscious. She took a deep breath as she looked at Sean. He was sitting on the gurney, his feet moving excitedly as if he were a child watching a much-awaited movie.

"Took you long enough to look up. I still exist, you know. Aren't you going to ask me what I want?" he asked giddily.

"You want me," Gillian said through sobs. "I know that."

"Gillian, you were always so naïve." Gillian wiped her tears as she watched Sean stand up. "You think I want what I wanted four years ago? Love dies, you know."

"Not true love," Gillian whispered.

"Cute, you love the dog. It's a dead dog now, you know."

"Will you kill Addie too?" she asked.

"And why not?" Sean sounded amused.

"She can't . . . I can't—" Gillian sank to the floor, her weeping getting the better of her.

"Can't what?" Sean walked towards her.

"I'm sorry."

"Oh, come on! This isn't the gal I knew. The one who wanted to live forever. The one I spent four years trying to find by refining our connection. You know how hard that was? Tell me, isn't immortality what you want now?" Sean roared. He grabbed her neck.

Gillian took as deep a breath as she could muster in her current position but did not take her eyes away from him. If she was going to die, she would do it without fear.

"You found me . . . after four years. Why now? What do you want from me Sean?" she asked, her hand grasping his, trying to loosen his hold from her neck. But she didn't remove her gaze from him. He could snap her neck at any time without effort. And while she welcomed this if her friends were no longer with her, she still had a glimmer of hope that Addie, being the strongest immortal in the room, at least at the present moment given Forrest's wound, would get up . . . somehow.

"Aren't you going to ask me how I'm controlling your movements, Gillian? A four-year-old connection is a powerful thing."

"So you learned a new trick. The connection has gotten more powerful over time. You found me. If you wanted revenge, you got it. Now let me go. If you don't want me, why keep me?" More tears streamed down her face. *I will be with you soon, Forrest. I will see you, Addie. You're with Mom now.*

"Why not?" Sean snickered. "Now that I've taken everything you hold dear, now that you have nothing to live for, perhaps you'll get a small chance to feel what I do. So, stay here, why don't you." He threw her to the floor, her knees stinging in pain once more. "Stay with your dog!" As she groaned in pain, she felt Forrest's body against hers. "It's time you learned your lesson. And when I'm done, and you're begging for me to strip the life out of you, I'll savor the blood, trickle by trickle. After all, it is not every day you get to kill the one who made you. Eric did all the technicalities, of course, but since it was your idea, you're the real maker. You're my maker."

"I'm sorry!" she screamed back. "I'm sorry I made you what you are! But most of all, I'm sorry I didn't kill you when I had the chance. I should've killed you right after you turned. I should've known your possessiveness and petty jealousy would get more powerful in your undead years."

"Oh, are you going to kill me now, witch? Fat chance, given I can control your movements. . . . But just to amuse you, I'll go with it. But know this: killing me will never bring back the ones you love."

Suddenly, Gillian knew what she had to do.

"You can't," she murmured. "But I can."

Chapter 37

"Sorry, love, didn't quite catch that. You? How can you stop a silver dagger? If you don't take it out, the silver will finish him. After all, we both know silver is fatal to werewolves, no? If you do, he'll bleed out. My, what a quandary you find yourself in! So, you might as well say your goodbyes now."

"You're right, Sean. Goodbye," Gillian whispered. She turned to Forrest.

"Hold on," she whispered, putting her right hand directly on top of the dagger. She was satisfied to discover he still had a pulse, although a very weak one.

Help me, Mom, please.

She squinted as she removed the dagger.

Forrest's right leg moved as though a muscle spasm was running through it. But she knew better.

I know it hurts. It won't be long now.

Gillian took off her scrub top, leaving on just her light tank top, as she tried, with futility she knew, to control the bleeding. She was able to discern that now the crimson liquid appeared a brilliant, almost shiny, shade of red.

Silver.

The blood had already mixed with the metal. She could not save him, but hopefully she could buy a few minutes before his soul would leave his body.

"If he's going, then so are you," Gillian said as she threw the dagger at Sean. She was not a precise shot, but her magic could land the dagger where she wanted it.

Finally.

Sean cried out as the dagger caught him in his right side, and blood began flowing out.

"Bitch! You ruined my favorite shirt!"

"You won't need it where you're going, you bastard," Gillian huffed, her right hand raising as she pinned Sean's body against the wall of the surgical suite.

Sean moaned in pain. Although Gillian had no time to lose, she was aware of how good it felt, despite the toll it was taking on her now. She could not deny the fatigue she suddenly felt just from holding the struggling vampire against the wall. But the feeling of finally having Sean within her grasp surely beat out her rise in blood pressure and the feeling of weakness.

"You'll pay for this, witch!" Sean growled.

"I've paid enough," Gillian said.

Her right hand turned into a fist as she pulled the silver dagger out of Sean's body.

"Argh!" He moaned in pain as he fell to the floor.

"Oh, so that's why you don't mess with sharp objects?" Gillian asked, taking deep breaths as she willed her body to keep the magic flowing just a little longer. "I thought the undead knew how to deal with pain. Physical pain, at least." Gillian took the silver dagger by the handle. "Oh well. I can spare you screaming some more, Sean, finally."

"We don't like to be reminded of what living is like," Addie said, making Gillian gasp as she saw the vampire behind her. "But direct sunlight, it really messes with our complexion you know." Addie pushed Gillian back as she took a still surprised Sean by the neck.

"My own scalpel? That's low. Even for you," Addie told him. "Now, stay away from my daughter." Addie grunted as she pushed him against the window blinds.

"Addie, I have to—"

"I'll take care of him, Gillian. Be with Forrest—he could use your comfort."

Gillian pushed her hair out of her face. She should have taken care of Sean. After what she was planning to do, it would be too late.

But the clock was also ticking for Forrest.

She dashed back to him and managed to get his body to face hers. She could detect no breathing. Hopefully, there was a pulse left.

She took his hand and put it against her heart.

"Don't worry, Forrest. You'll be back soon."

*"Ego tibi vitam do
anima pro anima.
Meam vitam ego do
Suscipe eam
meo cum amore.*

I give you life.
A life for a life.
My life I give you.
Take it from me, with my love."

"Gillian, no!" Addie's scream sounded distant.

Gillian gasped as she suddenly felt so weak that her knees gave out.

It worked!

She smiled as she heard Forrest draw a big gasp of breath.

Just when she started to feel out of breath herself.

She fell to the ground on her back as soon as she saw Forrest's gray eyes squinting to the light.

"Gillian? Gillian! Can you hear me? Oh, please…" There was Addie's voice again. And Gillian could swear she saw the cloudy reflection of her friend as she felt herself letting go.

Take care of him . . . and yourself, Addie.

"Say yes," said Addie urgently.

Chapter 38

"**G**illy, wake up honey."

Gillian moaned as she forced her eyes to open, gasping as she saw who was directly in front of her.

"Mom!" She hurriedly took the covers from her body, her stockinged feet looking for her baby-blue carpet on her bedroom's floor.

"Save your strength honey—you'll need it. You can stay where you are." Bridget moved toward her, taking her hand and sitting by her feet.

"Mom, did I summon you? I don't remember." She loosened her hold on her mother's hand once she realized how tightly she was holding it. But she had waited four years for this moment. She refused to let go. Was this a dream?

"No dear, I came on my own. It's about time." She could see tears in her mother's light green eyes as she went to stroke her daughter's cheek. "Oh, you're so beautiful."

"So, are you Mom." Gillian put her mother's other hand on her face, sobbing quietly.

"Oh, honey." Bridget took her into her arms. "I'm so sorry."

"Why didn't you come when I called you?" Gillian whispered through her tears.

"Because I could see you were still grieving. If I had come, you would have thought I was back. That isn't the case Gilly. I can't come back."

"But you can cross through magic."

"Magic can only do so much. I wasn't going to take away your lifeforce, Gilly. Of course, I wasn't counting on you giving it away, my girl. You must really love him." Gillian furrowed her eyebrows. Yesterday was so foggy in her mind. "No worries, you'll find out shortly. But now you must really trust Adelaide. This is uncharted territory, but if anyone can do it, it's you two. Or you three, I should say."

"What?"

"Gilly honey, you died. That is why I'm here. Addie saved you, but that doesn't come without consequences. You're now living in a borrowed lifeforce."

Gillian gasped, distancing herself from her mother. "Am I—"

"You're still my daughter Gillian, still a witch. You'll get through this."

"But—"

"Adelaide will be with you every step of the way. As will I. You may not be able to see me, but—"

"Mom, can't you stay?" She took her mother's hands again, afraid to let go. Once she let go, there was nothing to keep her mother from disappearing once more. Would she allow her to see her again?

"You know I can't Gilly. But I will always be with you. I always have been, make no mistake."

"Are you with Papa now at least?" she asked. She might as well get all the bad news out of the way at once.

"Gilly, your father is alive. I know he is. He'll find you soon enough."

Gillian put her mother's hands in her face again, marveling that, unlike Addie's, her mother's hands were soft and warm. Maybe she hadn't seen her father in heaven yet. She figured it was a big place.

"Okay, Mom," she whispered, inhaling her mother's all too familiar lavender scent. Oh, how she had missed that! How she had missed her!

Her brows furrowed once again as she saw a shadow near her bed, suddenly recognizing Addie's voice.

"She's still out? Shit, she's supposed to have awakened hours ago!"

"Calm down Addie, give her time. She will."

Along with Forrest's soft, calm one.

Instantly, her heart felt like thumping out of her chest. Her mother let out her musical laugh. Gillian sighed. She couldn't remember the last time she had heard her mother's laugh.

"Go on Gilly, wake up. He needs you. They both do."

"But I need you, Mom! I can't do this without you," Gillian admitted, letting out a breath she didn't know she was holding. She always thought she would be embarrassed to admit that, that she would never be as strong a witch, as strong a woman, as her mother was.

"Oh, I think you can, dear. You've been doing it all these years."

"And learning the hard way, Mom. How long can I keep this up?"

"As long as it takes Gilly. You stop learning, you stop living."

"Stay with me Mom, please," Gillian lay her hand in her mother's lap. "I miss you."

"I miss you, my Gilly. But you'll be fine. And I'll be looking down, always taking care of you. Never forget."

"Gillian, wake up, please!"

Gillian jumped out of her mother's lap, feeling herself shaking, and she distinctively heard Addie yell.

"Addie, this won't help. Take a breath. I'll call you if anything changes."

She once again heard Forrest intervene.

Her mother's hand went to her cheek once more.

"Go," she whispered.

"No, Mom, please don't go," Gillian sobbed once more.

"I love you Gilly. And try to stay off magic for a while. Your borrowed lifeforce won't appreciate it."

Epilogue

"**H**ey, beautiful."

Gillian flinched as she felt a warm hand caressing her cheek.

"I know, I'm sorry to wake you, but you have to eat something. And soon."

Gillian couldn't suppress a yawn as she forced her eyes to open. The first things she encountered were those dark gray eyes in the light stream of light that her room's heavy purple curtains allowed in.

"Forrest?"

"There she is, the woman who saved my life. You didn't have to do that, you know."

"Yes, I did. I couldn't lose you too," Gillian said softly, her hand going up to caress his cheek.

She winced as she felt how sore she was. It felt like she had overdone her workout at the gym by about two hours. She had never done that before. She had never even gone to the gym unless gym class in high school counted.

"Yes, you have to take it easy for a while, love. And after you feed, you can go back to bed."

"Feed?" That word was enough to make her suddenly sit up in bed, soreness be damned. Her mind went back to what her mother told her, but still, hadn't that been a dream?

"Now, Gillian—"

"Catch!"

Gillian gasped as she found a thermos in her right hand.

She seldom ever caught something on the first try. Even with all she'd picked up from her immortal friends, her coordination left a lot to be desired.

She looked at Addie leaning against the doorframe.

Addie shrugged, smiling. "You gave me no choice, you know. After all, I had a promise to keep."

Gillian should have understood what that meant. After all, just looking at the thermos made her stomach grumble. But she couldn't put it into words.

"Drink up. We'll talk later. I'll teach you everything you need to know, I promise," Addie told her in an assuring voice Gillian could not remember hearing before. She knew Addie was trying to calm her. But she had so many questions.

"My magic?" She finally was able to get one of the most important ones to the surface.

"I haven't changed you in any significant way. Everything you are is still there. Just that your eyes are open while your heart is not beating. It will take a while, but we'll get there. Go ahead, drink. You'll feel better."

Addie sat at the foot of the bed as Gillian opened the thermos, smiling at her cat next to the pillow. Dagonet was looking at her curiously.

"By the way, although I am thankful Forrest is here with us, pull something like that again and you'll never hear the end of it," Addie added, winking at her.

"Really, Addie?" Gillian looked at her friend as she put the thermos down. She would never admit it out loud, but she could not deny just how satisfied drinking its contents made her, and now, how powerful she felt. "Am I not one of you now? I'm sure I can take you on. Oh jeez!" Gillian gasped at her sudden outburst. "I'm sorry, I didn't mean that."

"Yes, you did. No worries. I'm not mad. A vampire's confidence and newfound ego is something to be reckoned with." She put her hand on Gillian's shoulder, taking the thermos away from her.

"I'm sorry."

"Don't worry, Gillian. I'll be with you every step of the way."

"Me too," Forrest chimed in.

"It'll be a learning experience . . . for all of us," Addie continued.

"Thanks, Addie." Gillian smiled, yawning afterwards. She suddenly felt very tired.

"Sleepy, are you? Sleep is crucial during the first few days as the body gets used to your new way of life. Sleep, and I'll be here when you wake up," Addie assured her, getting up from the bed.

"Get some rest." Forrest got up as well. But Gillian did not let him walk two steps before grasping his arm.

"Will you stay?" At this point, she didn't care about Addie's giant smirk.

Forrest sat down again, kissing her now cold hand. "Always."

CPSIA information can be obtained
at www.ICGtesting.com
Printed in the USA
LVHW031051110119
603522LV00005B/8